THE PROMISE OF BETHLEHEM

THE PROMISE OF BETHLEHEM

An Advent Nativity Story

Brian Elliott

Ariana Madison

SCHOCKWAVE
PUBLISHING

**SCHOCKWAVE
PUBLISHING**

Published by SchockWave Publishing Co, LLC.
975 E Riggs Rd
Ste 12-308
Chandler, AZ 85249 USA

The Promise of Bethlehem

First Edition: November 2025
Paperback ISBN: 979-8-9931982-9-3
Hardcover ISBN: 979-8-9931982-1-7

Written by Brian Elliott
Illustrations by Ariana Madison
Edited by Brooke Madison

SOLI DEO GLORIA

For Andrew
See ya till then!
-Daddy

FROM THE AUTHOR

I am so excited you have chosen to read *The Promise of Bethlehem.* Advent is the season of hope, excitement, and preparation for the celebration of Jesus's birth and to actively look forward to His promised return. It is during this time, I invite you and your entire family to prepare for Christmas by experiencing the heart of the Christmas story together—learning about the birth of our Lord and Savior, Jesus Christ, and the ultimate promise He fulfilled for humanity. This book is designed to help families not only celebrate the season, but also to reflect on the profound love and sacrifice of God *through* Jesus Christ.

Make no mistake, the Bible is the ultimate source of truth and should be read regularly to gain the wisdom and courage to follow Christ, but *The Promise of Bethlehem* is for the family—to build lasting habits of reading, praying, and engaging with the Bible together throughout the year. These practices strengthen family bonds, foster early childhood development, enrich faith, and create a shared foundation of love and spiritual growth. With its focus on the stories surrounding Jesus's birth, this book seeks to guide families toward a deeper relationship with God, revealing how God takes what seems to be a bad situation and uses it for good.

Merry Christmas!

CONTENTS

DECEMBER 1
The Big Task

Heaven is a place where kindness bubbles like a spring, where peace flows like a river, and love is as vast as an ocean. Its blue sky stretches endlessly with fluffy white clouds gently tickled by the peaks of tall mountain tops. The clouds laugh with a playful rumble, and they sprinkle with joyful rain down to the ground below. Lush green grass and the emerald-topped trees wait patiently to soak up the goodness that comes from above. And beautiful flowers add the final touches to the masterpiece designed by a faithful Creator who makes us yearn for more. God is so good, He knows just what we need!

Surrounded by the serene landscape is a city lined with streets of gold, fountains that flow with sweet honey, and buildings constructed of the finest wood, stone, and marble. Every inch of the city is clean and pure, just like those who call Heaven home. The saints, who once lived on Earth and followed God's rules, now find their peace in this paradise. And the angels, loyal helpers and messengers for God, who make sure His will be done on Earth as it is in Heaven.

Many years ago, God called upon a very special angel named Gabriel. He was young, but a dependable and faithful servant for the Lord. God had asked Gabriel to deliver many important messages before, but this time, the young angel was to deliver the biggest, most important message of all!

Gabriel loved to go to the topmost peak of Heaven to pray—it was his favorite spot. From there, he could see *all*

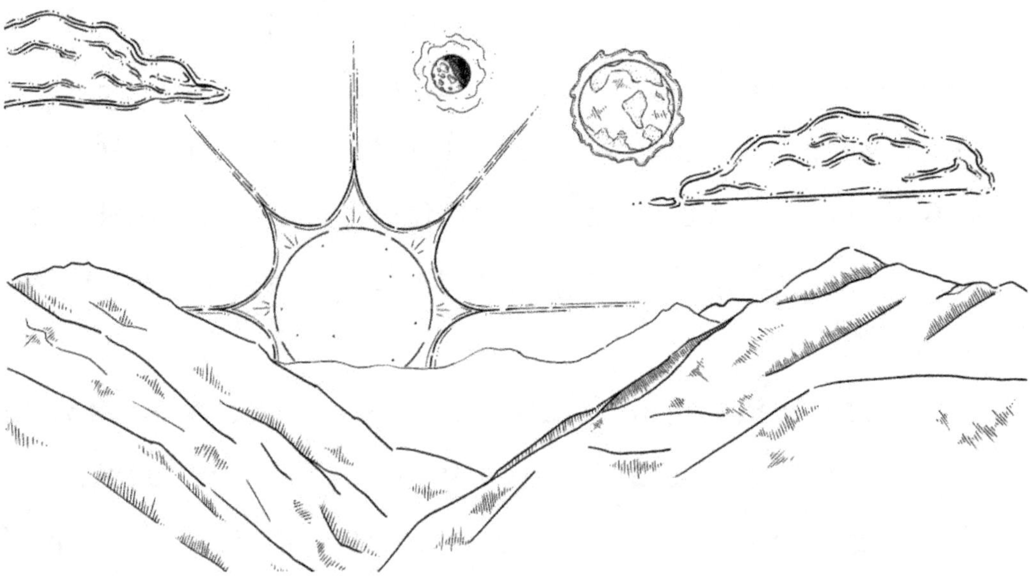

of God's creation: the sky, the mountains, and the valley below. But the thing that amazed him most, was the graceful dance between the Earth, Moon, and Sun. The bright blues and greens of Earth, the yellows and reds of the warm Sun, and the shades of grays and whites of the Moon all spun in perfect harmony.

I am so blessed to be here, Gabriel thought to himself. *God has perfectly created Heaven and the Earth. Surely there is nothing more for Him to do.*

"Gabriel!" a rumbling voice called out to the young angel, echoing like thunder from a distant storm.

It was GOD! The sound of God's voice made the tips of Gabriel's wings flutter with excitement. "Yes, Lord, I am here for You," he replied, jumping up off the ground, bubbling with glee.

"You have been a good and faithful helper, and I have a special task for you." God's voice was clear and full of power.

Gabriel stood in silence, taking in every word God spoke.

"It is time for Me to show the people of the world how much they mean to Me, how much I love them, and how far I am willing to go to show them My love. I need

you to deliver a message to a sweet girl in Nazareth named Mary."

Gabriel continued to look at God in amazement, His presence filled Gabriel's spirit. "I would be honored to do this for You, my Lord!"

"With My hands, I will plant My seed, My son, Jesus, in Mary's womb. If she is willing to accept Him, He will live on Earth to bring peace to the nations and save those who should be with Me in Glory forever. He is the Messiah I promised so long ago. Now go, tell her, and rejoice."

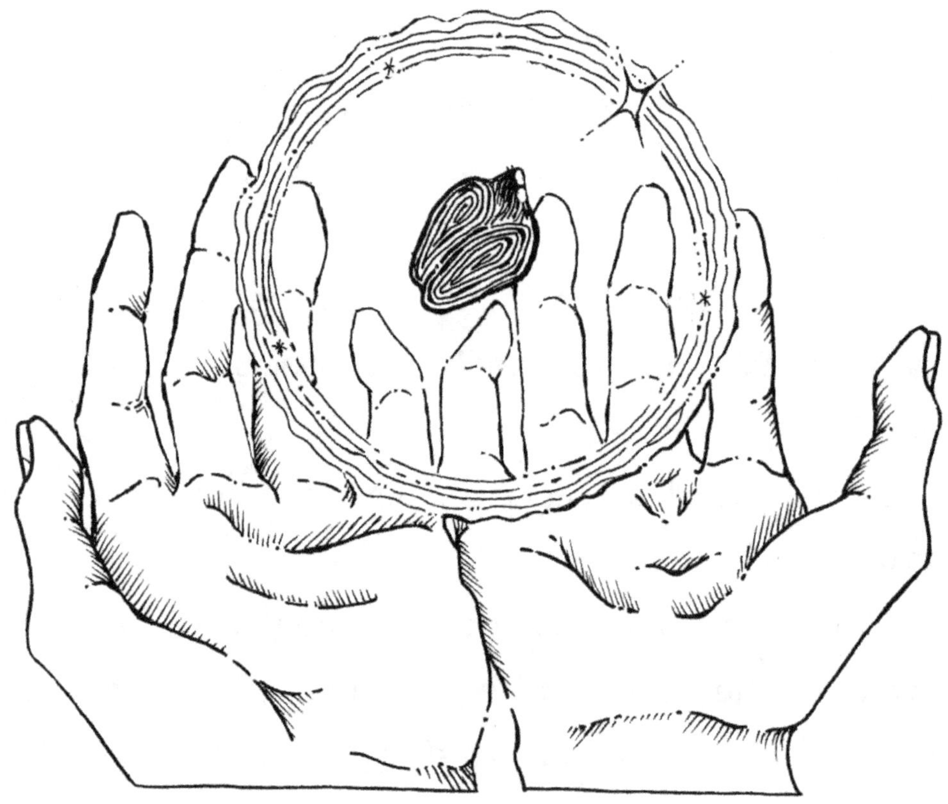

"Yes, Lord, I will go right away," Gabriel responded.

With the presence of God still flowing through Gabriel's spirit, he felt great excitement, but great responsibility. He didn't want to disappoint God with this big task.

It was time for Gabriel to go to Earth. He reached his arms out and opened his wings, stretching them as far as he could. He bowed his head and closed his eyes. The presence of the Lord continued to grow inside of him. He took a deep breath and said, "I am ready to serve You, Lord."

In an instant, the fabric of Heaven shifted around him, tearing a swirling hole into the sky. Gabriel and the other angels called it the *Eye of Heaven*.

The Eye of Heaven was a window they used to see what was happening on Earth. It was also a doorway to travel between the two realms. When opened, it pulsed and hummed with a deep drone of pure energy only God Himself could produce.

With light spiraling around Gabriel, the bright particles merged into themselves to reveal an image of Nazareth, then a garden, then a girl kneeling. *This must be Mary,* Gabriel thought looking into the Eye. *This is where I need to go.* And so, he would.

Gabriel raised his hands, looked to the Eye, and leapt into the air with the force of a hurricane. He lifted up off the ground, flew through the ring of light, and was delivered to Nazareth in the twinkle of an eye. A journey he had taken many times, but this time, it bore the weight of a *very* important message.

JOHN 3:16-17

"[16] For God so loved the world that he gave his one and only Son, that whoever believes in him shall not perish but have eternal life. [17] For God did not send his Son into the world to condemn the world, but to save the world through him."

DECEMBER 2
A Surprise in the Garden

It was a perfect spring morning and only a faint memory of winter was left in the air. With the emerging rays of sunlight, the town of Nazareth started to wake.

The men raced to the market to open their businesses, competing to see who could set up their shop first, while the women looked on unamused, simply wanting to get started with their day.

While others rushed to the market, Mary didn't like to participate in the morning spectacle. Her first commitment was to the Lord. She walked past the market to the opposite side of town where off the busy street and behind a brick wall, sat a quiet garden for her to pray to God.

With not a single person in sight, it was *her* secret garden, a hidden paradise tucked away in the middle of the dry desert. Other areas of town were caked in a hazy layer of what seemed to be a lingering dust cloud, but the garden was somehow free of the gritty air. It had beautiful, vibrant flowers just beginning to bloom, tall trees with branches that reached toward the sky, and fluffy, lush green grass that carpeted the ground—a perfect slice of heaven. To Mary, this garden didn't just look beautiful; it felt like home.

Mary knelt down in the grass and bowed her head. She weaved her fingers together, her hands clasped tight; she imagined she was holding God's own hand. Then she began to talk to God as if she was talking to a friend.

With her eyes closed, Gabriel descended from the Eye, which landed him quietly behind some bushes without being noticed. He pushed branches off to the side to peek through and see her. He watched her pray, just waiting for the right moment to approach her. He didn't want to frighten her but he wanted to make sure she knew he was God's helper. Excitement sparked in Gabriel yet again. *I can't wait to tell Mary about Jesus*, he thought to himself.

With a flash, Gabriel appeared in front of Mary, and in a voice as bold as he could muster, he said, "BEHOLD, I am a messenger for THE Almighty God! HE has sent me to tell you some good news!"

Mary jumped and gasped in surprise at Gabriel's sudden appearance. "You scared me!" she was finally able to say. Her voice was as shaky as her hands, which were now hovering over her lips. "I thought I was here alone."

"I am sorry I scared you, Mary, but do not be afraid," Gabriel continued, but this time in a softer tone. "God has heard your prayers and knows that you love Him very much. If you are willing, God has chosen you to be the mother of His only Son."

Confused by what she just heard, Mary responded, "But I am not married yet. How can I have a child?"

"The Holy Spirit will come upon you and a *very* special baby will begin to grow in you. Like the gardener who planted a tiny seed in this garden, and it grew into a perfectly made plant, you too will receive this gift," Gabriel tried to clarify.

"I am honored He has chosen me to do this, but I am engaged to marry Joseph. What is he going to think?" Her eyes widened.

"Do not worry, you are so precious to God and He will take care of you both. Rejoice! His name is Jesus, and He will be the Savior of the world—the Messiah that was promised to you and your family, so long ago."

Mary closed her eyes, and a tear escaped, running down her cheek, and fell onto the grass beneath her. But the tear was not one of sadness, it was one of joy and excitement.

She smiled and cried out, "Yes, I would love to be the mother of God's son. Let His will be done!"

As she said this, a light breeze blew through her head scarf. It was touch from God, breathing life into her.

Gabriel nodded with an accepting smile, and just as fast as he appeared, Mary's messenger from God, was gone.

LUKE 1:35

"The angel answered, 'The Holy Spirit will come on you, and the power of the Most High will overshadow you. So the holy one to be born will be called the Son of God.'"

DECEMBER 3
Heartbreak in the Market

Gabriel arrived back in Heaven and continued to watch over Mary through the Eye. His wings fluttered and a smile stretched across his face. He felt as though he had done a good job and wanted to see what happened next. Mary was still kneeling, her face cradled in her palms, and her breath escaped her lungs. Finally, she lifted her head. More tears rolled down her face, and Gabriel could hear her thoughts. *I must find Joseph and tell him what happened*. Her thoughts echoed through the mountains of Heaven.

Gabriel then considered, *Is she sad? Is she upset? I told her not to worry*. "God will take care of you!" he began to shout, but his voice didn't pass through the Eye. All he could do was continue to watch with hushed expectation.

She slowly lifted herself off the ground. Her legs were weak, wobbling under the weight of the words forming in her mind. *My sweet Joseph... he won't believe me, and now he won't marry me.* She continued to think as she walked out into the dusty marketplace.

God saw Gabriel's desire to go back, to remind Mary of what he said.

"Gabriel, you did well. She must do this through her own choice. We must be patient." God said calmingly.

Mary's steps were small, and her heart fluttered with butterflies. She walked through the crowds of merchants and customers to find her fiancé's booth where he sold his works. The market was filled with the sounds of haggling voices and animals that brayed, bleated, mooed, and clucked all around her. Finally, she could see Joseph. He was moving some boards out of his cart and into his tent when his eyes locked with Mary's. His smile was so irresistible, his hair was charming, and his eyes, kind. He was a good man, a man of God.

"Lord God, give me the words to say to Joseph. I don't want to hurt him, but this is Your will. I am so honored to bear Your child, and I want to do this *with* him." Mary prayed.

Heaven became weightless, and the air was joyful and bright with this prayer. God was pleased, but He knew what was to come next.

God and Gabriel watched as Mary approached Joseph.

Joseph's smile faded seeing the concern wash across Mary's face. And then she told him about her encounter with Gabriel and the message he had delivered.

"What do you mean the Holy Spirit has given us a baby?" Joseph asked, as trust drained from his body, and sadness flooded in. "This is just too hard to believe."

Mary tried to explain that they would take care of God's Son together, but he didn't allow her to finish. To Joseph, Mary had betrayed his trust, and this made him sad. So he quickly left, not giving his tears a chance to show. Mary stood there, alone by his booth, surrounded by the work of the man she loved.

Mary looked up to Heaven and began to pray again, "God, my trust is in You. You said You would take care of me *and* Joseph. So please, help him understand. Amen."

God heard Mary's plea and once more, sent a gentle gust of wind past her as a sign that everything would be okay.

Gabriel turned his gaze away from the Eye and looked to the bright presence of God above him. "God, do You need me to help show Joseph this is a gift from You?"

"Yes, I will have you help Joseph, but first I need you to go back in time one thousand years to meet with a shepherd in Bethlehem. He loves what I love, he trusts in Me, and follows My ways. He is a man after My heart and I am fulfilling a promise I made to him."

The Eye opened once more above Gabriel's head. The shifting of time was happening right before his eyes. He was filled with God's power. His feet lifted off the ground as he reached toward the bright swirling light. Then Gabriel's body was washed in light, and in an instant, he was taken to a time long before.

PROVERBS 3:5-6

"⁵ Trust in the Lord with all your heart and lean not on your own understanding;
⁶ in all your ways submit to him, and he will make your paths straight."

DECEMBER 4
An Age Before Christ

Like lightning cracking through the sky, God transported Gabriel to Bethlehem, one thousand years in the past. Before him, he saw a countryside of hills. Some were tall, others rolled easily into the next. The landscape was like a painting, with light green strokes of grass and brush, brown patches of dirt and rock, and a dancing blue stream weaving its way into the distance. A sprinkle of white wool scattered the land—sheep, grazing on the grass. There were small trees dotted around, but the largest one, on top of the highest hill, caught Gabriel's eye. It reminded him of his favorite spot in Heaven, a perfect place to think; where is that shepherd God wants him to find?

He started walking toward the tree. Gravity on Earth made Gabriel's weight feel heavy, especially marching up a hill. As Gabriel got closer, he could hear a *bloop* sound. A boy, resting against the tree, was tossing stones into the stream below. Gabriel walked closer and was about to introduce himself, when the boy heard the crunch from the dirt and grass below Gabriel's feet.

The boy whipped around, ready to release the stone gripped between his fingers. He was expecting a wild animal, a beast hungry to eat his sheep. But to his relief, it was just another boy approaching him. His head cocked to the side and his eyes narrowed, studying Gabriel. Even though he couldn't see Gabriel's wings, he knew there was something special about this boy.

Gabriel's hands flew up, showing he didn't have anything in them—he wasn't a threat. "Hello," Gabriel began. "I saw you sitting here and I thought I would come and say 'hi' to you."

The boy's heart raced and his breath trying to catch up. After his suspicious glare swept over Gabriel, his eyes softened and he responded, "Hi." He dropped the rock, placed his now empty hand across his chest, and began to laugh, "You scared me."

Gabriel smiled back. Relieved, he said, "I've gotten that a lot lately. Can I sit with you?"

"That would be just fine. I would love the company," the boy said to Gabriel, patting the ground inviting him to sit. "I'm David," he continued, "I was just taking a break from herding my flock. It's hard work being a shepherd."

Gabriel knew immediately this was who God wanted him to talk to. His wings, still hidden from David, fluttered with excitement. He introduced himself and told his new friend he was traveling to deliver a message to a friend. Little did David know, *he* was the recipient of the divine message. Gabriel just didn't quite know what the message was yet, but God always gave him the words he needed, when the time was right.

The two boys continued to watch the sheep graze and David told Gabriel stories about his family, his love of poetry and music, and fighting off bears, wolves, and mountain lions to save his sheep. "God was with me, and He gave me the strength to free my sheep from the grips of their jaws!" David's hands were flying through the air, acting out each scene with vigor. "That was the last time they ever tried that!"

The stories were exciting and Gabriel wanted to hear more, but David was cut off by the distant sound of one of his older brothers calling for him. The brother's voice was too far away to make out the words.

"Come closer, I can't hear you!" David shouted back.

The brother was running over the ridge from the direction of their house, across the grassy hills to where David and Gabriel were sitting. When he finally mustered enough energy to make it to the top of the hill, he hunched over at the waist, bracing his hands on his knees to catch his breath.

"I said..." he started again, "There's an old man here named Samuel." His voice was ragged as he choked out each word. "Father said he's a prophet... he can actually hear God's voice... and He has a message for one of us." He paused longer to focus on if breath.

David's eyebrows raised, eagerly waiting for his brother to finish. "And...? Tell me more!"

His brother stood up straight and looked at David, "The message wasn't for me—it's for you."

David and Gabriel looked at each other. They were curious and excited to know who this prophet Samuel was and what message he had for David.

David jumped to his feet and started running as fast as he could toward the house with Gabriel close behind. They weaved in and out of the sheep, leaving his brother behind, as they raced over the hills toward the small house made of mud and stone.

As the two boys neared the house, David saw his family gathered around an old man with a beard and walking staff. *That must be Samuel*, he thought to himself.

As David ran to the group, Gabriel returned to his spirit form. David didn't even notice his new friend was gone, his eyes were fixed on the old man.

He was a traveler. The sandals on his feet were worn and his robe and head covering were no longer white, but discolored from earth and sweat. His long beard appeared as white as a cloud against the background of the off-colored cloth.

The prophet's wrinkled face lit with excitement after finally locking with David's eyes.

"Yes!" Samuel's tired and old voice pushed with joy. "*You* are the one I have been searching for."

David didn't know it, but Gabriel was still with him, standing right behind him. He was glowing. His spirit shone brightly through David like the sun. Only Samuel could see this because he was God's prophet, but this was God's message and why Gabriel was sent to meet David.

Samuel walked over to David, awestruck by the sight that was revealed to him. In his hand he held a horn filled with oil. He lifted the vessel above David's head and began to pour out the warm glistening fluid. It flowed onto the crown of his head and down his hair. The air had cooled the oil and gave David an awakening purpose with every tap as it dripped onto his shoulders.

Samuel stepped back and marveled at the shepherd boy, "Our blessed Lord has chosen you to be the next King of Israel. Praise be to God!"

The mountains of Bethlehem sang in a silent worship, and David's family was in shock. But David heard Samuel's words echo in his mind, *King of Israel!* One day, he would be a king!

1 SAMUEL 16:13

"So Samuel took the horn of oil and anointed him in the presence of his brothers, and from that day on the Spirit of the Lord came powerfully upon David."

DECEMBER 5
The Promise

Before he could begin to process what had just happened, a blinding light flashed in front of Gabriel's face—the Eye of Heaven was opening again. The light from the Eye pulled him in; the sky lurched above his head. No one else, not even Samuel, could see or feel this—only Gabriel. When the twisting momentum around him slowed and the ground became still once more, he found himself in a new place—somewhere different—some *time* different.

When the glow from the Eye dimmed, it was dark, much darker than the midday sun outside David's house where he just was. Night had come and he was now inside a grand palace of limestone walls, cedar wood beams, with paintings and treasures throughout. It was dark in the room where Gabriel now stood except for a flame flickering in a fireplace on the other side of the room. Two men stood in front of the fire, their backs were to Gabriel.

Gabriel walked toward the men and could hear them having a conversation with each other, but he was much too far away to make out what they were saying. Gabriel continued to move closer. Finally he could see the men. One was dressed in royal clothing, with a crown on his head and a blue sash etched with gold rested across his shoulder. The other was in a plain tunic and a cloth draped over his head. They were speaking gently to each other, as if they

cared for one another. Gabriel was now close enough to hear what they were saying.

"God has provided this beautiful palace for me and my family. I am so thankful... I want to dedicate something to Him in return," the man with the crown said. "I would like to build a grand temple for the Lord."

The other man nodded, a broad smile stretching across his face, and responded enthusiastically, "We should draw up plans right away!"

The man in the crown lit up with joy and started to walk out of the room. He then stopped, as if remembering he needed to say something. He turned back to his companion and said, "Nathan, thank you for being such a great advisor and a dependable friend."

"It is truly my honor, King David," Nathan responded.

Gabriel realized at that moment the man in the crown was his friend David, the shepherd boy he met in the field, but he was thirty years older, and now the King of Israel.

Gabriel was amazed and happy to see his friend again, but he had to stay focused—God had more for Gabriel to do.

The bold voice of the Lord came upon Gabriel once more, **"I do not want David to build Me a temple. He is a**

great warrior with a sense of leadership and responsibility over My beloved people, but now is not the right time," God said to Gabriel. **"Tell Nathan to stop this from happening."**

David was now gone but Nathan stayed to think and pray. The flickering orange glow highlighted Nathan's full cheeks, plump with a smile at the thought of the new project.

"Oh, Spirit of the Lord, I feel your presence," he prayed, unable to see Gabriel but sensing a Godly spirit was with him. Slowly, Gabriel revealed himself to Nathan and lit up the room completely. "Praise God!" Nathan said, raising his hands and eyes in worship.

"I am Gabriel," he responded clearly. "God has sent me to tell you a message. He does not want David to build His temple; his son will do this in *his* reign as king."

Gabriel felt a connection with God, as if He was talking directly through him. "But instead, God will build David a temple of everlasting life. The Messiah, the Savior of *all* people, will be born into his lineage, and His Kingdom will have no end. God loves David very much and He wants to reward him for his faithful devotion. Now go tell David this."

Nathan had received visions and prophecies before, but this was very different, and very clear. He nodded at Gabriel and walked quickly out of the room in search of King David to tell him the message.

God continued to talk to Gabriel. **"David is a wonderful man. He is a man after My own heart. He is not perfect, but it's his faith, his devotion, and his repentance I want to honor for all generations to come. Both Mary and Joseph are descendants of David. Through them, Jesus will be born. Now go, reveal this message to Joseph."**

Once more, the Eye swirled in front of Gabriel. He stepped into it and returned to Nazareth, standing outside of Joseph's workshop as the sun stretched its last rays of light. The blue sky was about to be covered by the blanket of night.

At the front gate, Gabriel found a lantern lying on its side. Still filled with oil, he lit it, and made his way up the worn dirt path to the entry of the tired building. Holding up the lantern, he pushed the door open and called out, "Joseph... I have a message for you."

2 SAMUEL 7:13

"He is the one who will build a house for my Name, and I will establish the throne of his kingdom forever."

DECEMBER 6
A Message for Joseph

Joseph pulled himself away from Mary. There was nothing more for him to say and anything he wanted to say wouldn't be nice. His legs pushed his feet onto the gravel with such force that they turned rocks into powder. The dusty streets turned red and his feelings were boiling with hurt just thinking about what Mary told him. He left his booth with all his merchandise but it didn't matter. Every step was one step closer to home, but a step further away from Mary, a distance that felt too far to fix.

Finally, he arrived at his house. Going inside would remind him of Mary. He had imagined her living and building a life there with him, but that would be no more. Instead, he walked to his workshop which sat behind the house.

Stepping through the door just as he did every day, he saw all the unfinished projects surrounding him—chairs, spoons, bowls, children's toys and now a life with Mary. Even his workshop reminded him of Mary. Sadness gripped Joseph's chest and tears raced down his cheeks. He loved Mary, but the thought of his beloved starting a family with someone other than him flooded his mind.

His feet shuffled through the bits of wood that carpeted the floor as he made his way to his workbench. Sunlight streamed through the windows and cracks in the walls, catching dust in the air and forming golden beams so thick he could almost grab them.

Sitting on top of the bench was a wooden mallet Joseph's father gave to him as a little boy. He wrapped his fingers around the handle, clenching it perfectly in his hands. Looking at the tool he was reminded to keep moving forward and do his best for the Lord—a message passed down from generations before him.

Joseph began to work on the projects that surrounded him. He hammered, sawed, and smoothed the edges with sandstone all afternoon. One after another, raw wood transformed into finished pieces of art.

The late sun was on the cusp of turning to dusk. Joseph was tired and still thinking about what Mary told him in the market. *The Holy Spirit...? A baby...? How can this be?*

Then a knock came at the door and it opened with a creak. A magnificent light flooded the room from the doorway. Unable to see who it was, Joseph held up one hand to block the light from his eyes. He heard a voice from behind the light call his name.

"Joseph, descendant of David, I have a message for you."

Joseph responded, "I can't see your face, please lower your lamp." It was not a lamp, but the brilliant glow from Gabriel's spirit.

"Don't be afraid to take Mary as your wife, because in her womb is a gift from the Holy Spirit. She will have a Son, and the Lord our God wants you to help her raise Him. You are to name Him Jesus," the young angelic voice said.

"Who are you?" Joseph asked, confused.

"My name is Gabriel. I'm an angel of God," Gabriel answered. "He has sent me to deliver this message to you."

"I can't believe this," Joseph said, both amazed and crushed with guilt. "Mary was trying to tell me this and I didn't listen."

"Joseph," Gabriel cut in, "don't worry. God has given you this great responsibility to raise His Son, not as a burden, but as a gift. He is the promised Messiah!"

Still bathed in the bright glow coming from Gabriel, Joseph fell to his knees, raised his hands to Heaven, and began to praise God.

"Lord God, thank you. I am Your servant, and I am honored to watch over Your Son, Jesus."
The light from Gabriel then started to dim like a flame at the end of its wick.

The warmth of the morning sun poked through one of the small cracks of the shop walls, hitting Joseph's face as it began to rise over the distant mountains.

He opened his eyes. "What a dream." He whispered, lifting his head off the bench where he slept. "I didn't even realize I had fallen asleep. I must go tell Mary about this and I hope she will still want to be my wife."

Without delay, Joseph ran over to Mary's house to apologize. He wanted to tell her that an angel of the Lord also visited him in a dream. But when he arrived at her house, he was too late. Mary had left, and he didn't know when she would return.

MATTHEW 1:20-21

"20 But after he had considered this, an angel of the Lord appeared to him in a dream and said, 'Joseph son of David, do not be afraid to take Mary home as your wife, because what is conceived in her is from the Holy Spirit. 21 She will give birth to a son, and you are to give him the name Jesus, because he will save his people from their sins.'"

DECEMBER 7
Mary Visits Elizabeth

Standing alone in front of Joseph's booth, Mary's mind was filled with a deafening silence. She watched Joseph walk away; he didn't even turn around. Mary thought something like this would happen, but she trusted God was working through her.

She had an overwhelming need to talk to someone. Her mom wouldn't understand, her dad might disown her, and Joseph? Well, he definitely didn't want to talk.

Mary thought for a bit, then it came to her. Elizabeth, her favorite cousin—she was expecting a child too! Surely, she would understand. Her small farm was in the mountains outside of Jerusalem, which would be many days of travel. Yes, it would be a tough journey, but it would give Mary a chance to clear her mind and give Joseph the space he needed.

Mary rushed home and told her parents she would be going to see Elizabeth and Zechariah. She gathered a few of her belongings and a little money for food and to pay for places to stay along the way. Then she set off on the long journey across the desert.

The road stretched endlessly before her. She traveled alone, on foot, making her way through the rocky hills and dry desert. The old dirt path wound through the sunbaked desert, each bend revealing more desert and more path to walk.

After many days of travel, Mary was getting close. One foot in front of the other, then finally the walls of the great city of Jerusalem were in view—a beacon in the desert marking just how close she was to finishing her journey.

"My Lord God in Heaven, continue to lift my feet and bring air to my lungs. Give me strength to push onward," Mary prayed. Her mood shifted from pure exhaustion to revived motivation seeing the ancient city ahead.

Mary continued to walk for a bit longer. She bypassed Jerusalem and went into the mountains. Then finally, after many long days of travel, her cousin's house came into view. The house was nestled between a ridge of mountains on a small plot of land. It was a quaint place made of clay brick and a flat roof. A small vegetable garden and pens for a few goats, some chickens, and a couple cows surrounded the house. She walked her last few steps up the long walkway made of stones they had likely collected from around the house.

The smell of food hit Mary's nose, then it settled into her stomach with a noticeable rumble. She knew Elizabeth loved to cook and she couldn't wait to eat a good meal.

Mary shuffled across the loose path up to the front door. Before entering, she looked up at the dusk-painted sky and whispered, "Thank you!" in gratitude.

She lifted her fist and knocked on the wooden door. Sounds of a working kitchen instantly stopped and were replaced with footsteps drawing closer to the entrance. Through a small opening in the door, Mary saw Elizabeth's face staring back at her.

"Zechariah, Mary is here!" Elizabeth's voice yelled back into the room, excited.

The door opened into the cozy home, and Elizabeth held a hand up to her lips as tears welled in her eyes.

"Oh, Mary, what a surprise! It is so good to see you," Elizabeth said, pulling Mary in for a warm embrace. "Even my little one in my womb is jumping for joy like I have never felt before."

Both women couldn't stop smiling.

"I am so happy to see you too," Mary said with little energy left. "I came all this way because I have to tell you something that cannot wait."

Elizabeth released Mary from her grip and took a step back, reaching for Mary's hands, "You can tell me anything, we are like sisters," she reassured her. "Although, I would be a *much* older sister." She smirked at Mary.

A puff of air escaped Mary's nose, and she curled her lip to form a small smile at the joke. It was all she could muster.

"Come in and sit. You must have had quite a journey to get here." Elizabeth closed the door behind Mary.

The two women walked into the small room. It was well lit with lanterns and the fire for cooking. They found chairs and a pillow for each to sit on. Mary felt a rush of relief as she sat down and was finally able to rest her sore feet.

Then Mary looked into Elizabeth's eyes, her face fell serious. She cleared her throat as her nerves began to flutter. With Joseph's reaction still fresh on her mind, she didn't want Elizabeth to think she was crazy or that she was trying to overshadow her cousin's pregnancy, but she had to tell her.

"I was visited by an angel, sent by God Himself," Mary began. "He told me I would bear God's Son and I am to name Him Jesus."

Elizabeth's eyes grew wide and a loud shout of happiness rippled through the house. She reached for Mary's hands again and was finally able to say, "Praise the Lord! Blessed are you among women! I am so honored to have the mother of our Messiah in my house."

"Thank you for not thinking I'm crazy," Mary said, relieved.

"Crazy?!" Elizabeth's brows rose and her eyes wandered across the room toward Zechariah sitting at the table then back at Mary. "Let me tell *you* a story. But first, I'll bring you some food. I'm sure you're starving!"

LUKE 1:42-44

"42 In a loud voice she exclaimed: "Blessed are you among women, and blessed is the child you will bear! 43 But why am I so favored, that the mother of my Lord should come to me? 44 As soon as the sound of your greeting reached my ears, the baby in my womb leaped for joy."

DECEMBER 8
Elizabeth and Zechariah

Elizabeth brought over two clay bowls of soup from the kitchen to where the ladies were sitting. Mary reached out for her bowl, then held it up to her nose. The steam rose and softly kissed her cheek like a faint memory of home. She closed her eyes and took in a deep breath. "Oh, this smells so good," she said, eager to eat.

The warm bowl tickled her hands as she looked down to see it was a lentil and vegetable soup with a slice of fresh baked bread emerging from the hot liquid. Bits of lentil, onion, garlic, and herbs swam in the rich brown broth, teasing Mary with the promise of comfort after traveling for so long.

Elizabeth sat down in her chair, raised her bowl with both hands and began to pray, "Oh blessed Lord, thank You for this food and thank You for bringing Mary to our home safely under Your hands of protection. Please use this food to nourish our bodies so that we may do Your will. Amen."

Mary echoed her amen and raised the bowl to her lips. Broth filled her mouth, exciting her tongue, giving her the instant sense of comfort she had hoped for.

A smile spread across Elizabeth's face as she watched Mary enjoy her dinner. They each took their time to eat and finally Elizabeth put down her bowl to tell Mary *her* story.

"So... I was cleaning the house," Elizabeth started, "when Zechariah came home from the temple. He didn't say a word to me, which is not like him. It was an extra special visit; he was chosen to burn incense in the sanctuary where the Spirit of the Lord is most present."

Mary looked at Elizabeth, trying to absorb every detail.

"I asked him, 'Aren't you going to tell me about your time at the temple? It's a great honor to be there, and you say nothing?' But something wasn't right. He actually couldn't speak."

Mary's eyes widened with curiosity.

"I was concerned but then he started writing down what had happened."

Elizabeth stood up and walked over to a small table. She returned with a letter and handed it to Mary. Mary put her bowl down, grabbed the letter, and began to read:

> I was in the temple, praying that we may have a child. I was burning incense and, in the haze, I started to see a boy appear, but it was no boy – it was an angel. I was scared, but he told me to not be afraid. Then he said God has heard my prayer. God is going to give us a child and we must name him _John.

Mary was astonished. She stopped reading for a moment and just looked at Elizabeth with her mouth open. Then she continued reading:

> I then asked the angel, how could this be? I am an old man, and well, you are also... well along in years.

Again, Mary stopped and looked at Elizabeth with her mouth open even wider. Elizabeth responded with an annoyed, "I know."

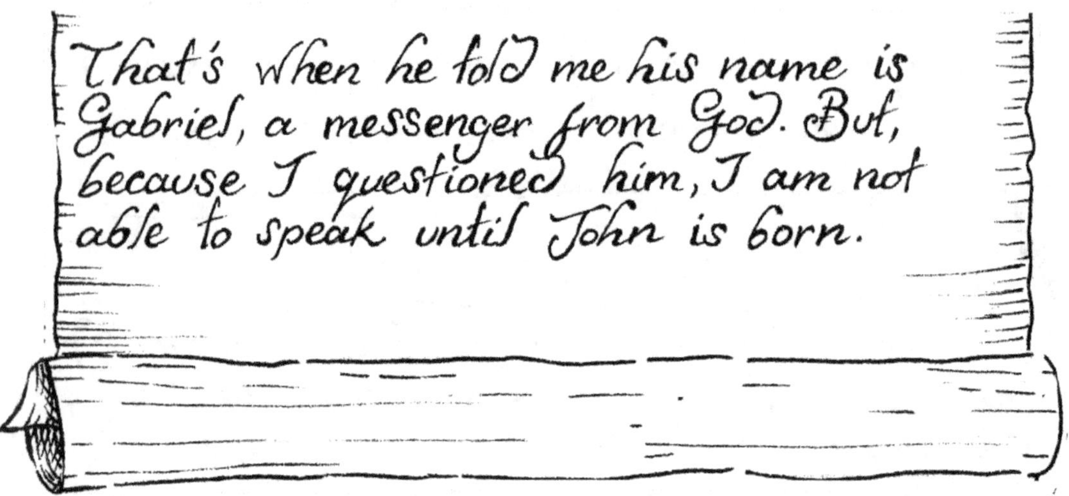

Mary blinked down at the letter and shook her head slowly in awe.

"The name of the angel that came to visit *me* was Gabriel," Mary wept in joy. "Thank you for sharing this with me."

"My little John has come to us to prepare the way for Jesus," Elizabeth replied gently.

The two stood up, hugged each other, and praised God.

LUKE 1:13-14

"¹³ But the angel said to him: 'Do not be afraid, Zechariah; your prayer has been heard. Your wife Elizabeth will bear you a son, and you are to call him John. ¹⁴ He will be a joy and delight to you, and many will rejoice because of his birth.'"

DECEMBER 9

John Is Born

Mary stayed with Zechariah and Elizabeth for a few months, helping around the house—cooking, cleaning, and going to the market in town. Mary wanted to make sure Elizabeth didn't overwork herself.

In the time she stayed, she grew even closer to her cousin. They laughed, told stories, and prepared each other for their new adventures as mothers. Then the day finally came for John to be born, just as Gabriel had said.

Elizabeth laid on a worn mat at the back of the house, where the room was dimly lit with lanterns set on old wooden barrels in the corners. On one side of Elizabeth was a midwife, providing instruction and words of encouragement. On the other was Mary, wiping her forehead with a damp cloth, holding her hand, and singing psalms to calm and ease her pain.

Elizabeth's breathing was fast, her heart pounded, and her stomach tightened with every passing minute. This was the toughest thing she ever had to do but she was so excited to welcome her baby boy into the family. She spent decades believing she would never have a child, and yet here she was, welcoming the son God had promised her. She is going to be a mother!

Waiting outside the room anxiously was Zechariah, along with other friends and neighbors who gathered to support the new family and witness the miracle unfold. Zechariah paced nervously, hanging on to every moment.

Then a cry pierced the air. The wail of the new born was the sound of a fulfilled prayer. Gently lifting the child, the midwife placed him in Elizabeth's arms. He was warm, his tiny chest rising and falling in quick, urgent breaths. Elizabeth's eyes focused solely on her baby boy, nothing breaking her gaze.

Mary just witnessed the power of God right before her eyes. It was a preview of what was to come. Joy flowed through her, still holding her cousin's hand and wiping her head.

The door to the tiny room finally swung open. There stood Zachariah, tears in his eyes. Still without words, he walked over to his wife's side and knelt down, placing his forehead against Elizabeth's and wrapping his arm around her.

A small audience formed at the door to get a glimpse of the newborn. Everyone gave shouts of congratulations and cheer.

One close friend shouted out joyfully, "We welcome this new boy into our community… Zechariah Jr!" for it was of tradition to keep a family name.

"No," Elizabeth said softly, still locking eyes with her son. "We want to name him John."

"Are you sure?" They questioned. "You have no one else in your family named this."

"NO!" came a booming voice from Elizabeth's side. It was Zechariah. "My son's name is John!"

Elizabeth slowly lifted her eyes toward Zechariah and relief spread across her face. Now *she* was unable to speak, not by divine command, but by pure amazement.

The room fell silent. Finally realizing he could speak again, Zachariah cried out to God, "Thank You my Lord, for You are good and merciful!"

Someone from outside the door said, "This family is truly favored by God!"

"This is a miracle!" said another.

Turning his gaze back to John, Zechariah gently placed a hand on his little head and said, "Our John will be a prophet, and God will speak through him to prepare our people for the best gift He has ever given us—Mary's boy, Jesus!"

Shortly after John was born, Mary knew she had to return to Nazareth. She was really missing Joseph, and she prayed Gabriel had revealed the message to him also.

She packed up her things and began the long journey home, this time with a group of travelers. As she got closer to home, she saw signs posted along her route by Roman soldiers:

LUKE 1:76-77

"76 And you, my child, will be called a prophet of the Most High; for you will go on before the Lord to prepare the way for him, 77 to give his people the knowledge of salvation through the forgiveness of their sins."

DECEMBER 10
Caesar Augustus

Looking down from atop the highest hill in the heart of Rome stood a magnificent palace. It was a brilliant sight to see. It had marble columns, doors carved from the finest wood, masterfully chiseled fountains trickling water, and birds that chirped around the beautiful estate. In the grand hall, the floors were white and polished to a mirror-like finish. The walls were decorated with large colorful murals and imposing statues of past Roman rulers. But beneath all its beauty, the spirit of Rome was not one of peace, but of power and pride.

Dressed in a red tunic and a golden crown of laurel, Caesar Augustus paced through the massive room. The steady rhythm of his footsteps echoed off the hard stone walls. Soldiers, trusted advisors, senators, and scribes all lined the room waiting for their leader to address them. The crowd was quiet, their attention unwavering.

Finally, he stopped as he reached a desk at the front of the room. Staring at a map of his empire sitting on the wooden top, Caesar bellowed, "We must grow the empire!" His voice, deep and commanding, reverberated throughout the hall.

Silence was the only answer. Any response opposing Caesar's would be bad news for the messenger. After some time, one of his generals stepped out of line and responded nervously, "Sir, in order to do so, we must train more soldiers."

Then a treasurer stepped forward and added, "We are also running out of money, Your Excellence. It will be *impossible* to hire new soldiers."

Augustus responded with his own silence. His face tensed, thinning his eyes to a squint. His neck and ears turned the same crimson color as his tunic.

Impossible? The word repeated in the emperor's mind, like a hyena's laugh, mocking his authority and ability. He glanced down at the map again and noticed a Roman coin lay beside it. He pulled the silver piece to the edge of the desk and picked it up, staring at it with piercing eyes. The treasurer over-estimated his influence. Making a fist, Caesar placed the coin on top of his thumb and began flipping it in the air.

Brrrring... catch...

Brrrring... catch...

The sharp metallic ring sliced through the tense silence, the cadence slow but deliberate. He tossed the coin into the air one last time, Brrrring... catch.

Clenching the coin in his fist, his sight fixed on the outspoken treasurer. Slowly he opened his hand to reveal the face of his father staring back at him.

"Do NOT tell me it is *impossible*!" He said, angrily slamming the coin on the desk. "We will tax the people to get the funds we need."

"But Your Excellence, we have already taxed the people of this land," the treasurer pleaded.

"Then we will tax the people MORE!" Caesar's voice shook the walls, thick with frustration. "I will require a census to make sure that I can get every bit of money out of them."

At once, the scratching of the scribes' pens filled the air.

Caesar's gaze swept the room before landing on a single scribe standing below the bust of his uncle, the same uncle on the coin.

"You!" he thrust a finger in the man's direction, "See that notices are written and posted at once. In six months, every citizen must return to their homeland for a census." His lips curled into a thin smile. "General, prepare for training. Oh, and find me a new treasurer... a position has just opened up."

Caesar turned his back as two soldiers carried out the treasurer, never to be seen again.

LUKE 2:1

"In those days Caesar Augustus issued a decree that a census should be taken of the entire Roman world."

DECEMBER 11
Mary Returns Home

It had been three months since Joseph left Mary at the market. She had left to see her cousin, and he never got a chance to apologize. He spent his time focused on his work, as the familiar movements of carpentry quieted the worry in his mind.

He was eager for her to get back. For weeks, the sound of every camel, ox, or donkey that passed by gave him hope that she was returning, but when he raced to see, it was not her.

At long last, a large group was arriving in town. The distinct bray of donkeys and the creaking of wooden wheels reached his ears. His hammer froze mid-swing. *Could it be?* he thought to himself, *Is she back?* A question he had asked himself many times, but this felt different.

Joseph quickly set his tools down and ran to the open doorway. The midafternoon sun stretched across the dusty road as the caravan slowed, approaching his house. His heart skipped. She was sitting next to the driver in a cart pulled by a donkey.

They moved slowly and deliberately. Joseph dashed to the street, hoping to encourage the driver to speed up. Coming to the edge of the road, he took a final, hesitant step forward, unsure if he should hug Mary or fall to his knees and apologize. She saw Joseph and smiled, waving at him with excitement. The others in the group continued to move forward but Mary's cart stopped where Joseph stood.

She smiled at the driver and said 'thank you' as if they were old friends. Then Mary stepped down from the cart, her hands brushed the folds of her robe and her face illuminated with light.

She had changed.

There was something in her eyes, a glow that hadn't been there before. Then he noticed... she *was* different.

The fabric of her dress rested against a small bump beneath it.

Joseph held out his hands, and Mary accepted his warm invitation. His stomach began to twist in knots as their eyes locked on each other.

"Hi," Mary said, but her thoughts raced with all the things she wanted to say to him.

Joseph could hardly say any words he was so nervous. "I have missed you so much," he paused and looked at the ground. "I am so sorry for the way I acted that day in the market. Now I know what a fool I was for not listening to you. I also had an angel visit me and he told me the Holy Spirit had come upon you, just as you were trying to explain to me in the market that day. *You are the mother of God's Son."* Joseph's eyes rose once again to meet with Mary's. "Could you ever forgive me?"

Mary's face softened and responded, "I would forgive you seventy times seven times. I missed you too."

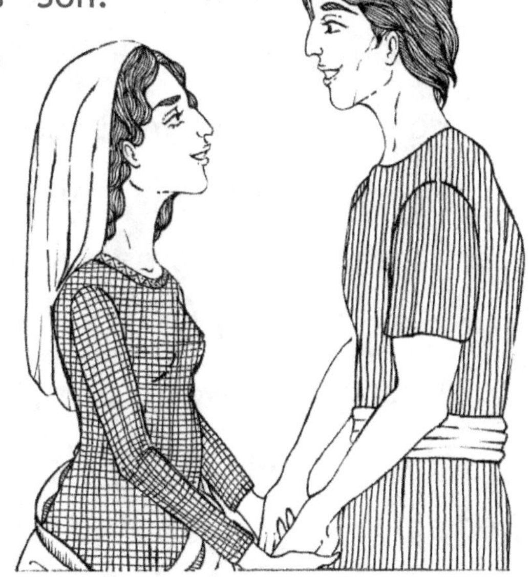

The couple locked in a hug, not letting go. It was a familiar embrace that now felt new again.

"I must tell you about my trip," Mary said.

"Yes, yes. Let's go in and tell me all about it," Joseph responded.

The two walked up the path and into Joseph's house. He asked Mary to sit at the table he had hand-crafted. He then grabbed two cups, filled them with fresh water, and set their drinks down in front of each of them.

Mary began to tell Joseph about her visit, his eyes fixed on her, absorbing every word. Happiness filled the room. It was cozy, familiar, and they were in love more than ever. She talked about her trips to the city, the fun they had cooking and playing games, but then she told him about Zechariah's visit from Gabriel.

Joseph was amazed at Elizabeth's story. "This is how she could have a child at such an old age; it is God's will!"

"Not only that—it's all connected," Mary explained. "John was born to prepare the way for our Jesus to be the promised Messiah!"

Joseph was awestruck by this, *the Messiah.*

They continued to talk into the evening. Then Mary remembered the sign she saw on the way back to Nazareth.

"As I got closer to home, I saw a sign being posted by the Romans. Have you seen it?" Mary asked.

"I have," Joseph replied, "and once we are married, you will need to come with me to Bethlehem, where my family is from."

"That's right," Mary started, "and what else will happen in six months?" Mary waited for just a moment—she batted her eyes and rubbed her stomach.

Joseph finally realized, and with wide eyes he could only say, "Oh, my!"

MATTHEW 18:21–22

"21 Then Peter came to Jesus and asked, 'Lord, how many times shall I forgive my brother or sister who sins against me? Up to seven times?' 22 Jesus answered, 'I tell you, not seven times, but up to seventy times seven.'"

DECEMBER 12
Preparing For Travel

More than five months had passed since Mary returned home from her trip to see her cousin. In that time, Joseph and Mary got married. It was a small but beautiful wedding, and all their family and close friends were there to celebrate with them. Mary was simply happy to finally be married to Joseph.

Soon the days grew shorter and the nights colder. The thought of traveling to Bethlehem raced through Joseph's mind.

"We only have a few nights left before we leave for Bethlehem," Joseph said with a bit of worry in his voice.

The dimly lit room was but a shadow of Joseph's concern. His elbows were on the wooden table supporting his body from completely falling over. His head was cradled in his hands. Any more thoughts of the things that could go wrong on their trip would certainly cause his hands to buckle under the weight and his head to join with the wooden top.

But Mary was not concerned, for God would take care of them. She looked down into the pot of stew she was cooking. She nodded, and sweetly replied, "Mmhm." She was not worried by the idea of traveling even though Jesus would be coming in a couple of weeks.

"How are you so calm right now?" Joseph continued. "We have to travel really far and you will be having Jesus soon. There will be lots of people heading to town, not just us." Joseph was increasingly panicked the more he saw Mary at ease. "Why are you not worried?" he asked again, nearly falling to his knees this time.

"My love, the only thing I am worried about right now is making sure I don't burn the bottom of our stew," she said, unfazed by his pleas of uncertainty. "We were both visited by Gabriel, and he told us not to be worried. So,

I'm not. We know Jesus is God's son; God is faithful and He will take care of us."

Mary then pulled the pot off the stove. She scooped a few heaping spoons of stew into two bowls, picked them up, and walked them over to Joseph.

"There!" she said with a sense of completion, "Dinner is served. Let's pray."

Joseph sat up and released his worry. They both held hands, bowed their heads, closed their eyes, and Joseph began to pray.

"Loving God, we thank You for this food You have provided for us. Just as You have provided us with food, please provide us with wisdom and safe passage as we travel. We love You. Amen."

Mary slowly raised her head, opened her eyes, and with a reassuring smile said, "Amen."

MATTHEW 6:25-26

*"*25 *'Therefore I tell you, do not worry about your life, what you will eat or drink; or about your body, what you will wear. Is not life more than food, and the body more than clothes?* 26 *Look at the birds of the air; they do not sow or reap or store away in barns, and yet your heavenly Father feeds them. Are you not much more valuable than they?'"*

DECEMBER 13
On the Road

The cool, crisp air settled over the still, small town of Nazareth, but the sun would soon rise, waking its people and fellow travelers. There were others leaving and yet others coming for the census Caesar ordered, so Joseph wanted to get an early start.

He was already outside preparing their donkey, who would carry Mary and their belongings to Bethlehem. In the dim light of dawn, Joseph buckled the last strap of the leather bridle and looked at the animal as if he was getting ready to talk to a friend.

"Okay, donkey, I have water, food, money, and our clothes. I think I have everything we need but I always feel like I am forgetting something." The journey would take over a week, and he didn't want to forget anything, especially with a new baby on the way.

At about that same time, Mary walked out of the house and onto the porch. She was glowing with excitement. She wore layers of clothes meant to keep her comfortable—warm while the sun sleeps, but cool when it awakens.

She called out to Joseph, her hands folded on her now fully formed stomach. "Are we all ready, love?" she asked. "You're talking to the donkey again, so we must be close." She snickered with delight.

Joseph smiled a wobbly smile and replied, "Yep, ready to go."

Mary stepped off the porch and walked down the path to join Joseph. Her gait gently swayed from one side to the other. "Did you remember to grab our identification?" she asked, with a knowing smirk.

Joseph smacked his forehead, trying to shove the idea back into his brain. He shook his head in disbelief. "I knew I was forgetting something," he responded, put out by his forgetfulness.

"Thought so," she said, still wearing a playful smile. "That's why I grabbed them." She pressed the papers into Joseph's chest and teased him with a light tap of her finger as she pulled away.

Joseph scrunched up his face and wobbled his head back at Mary as she strutted past to mount the donkey. He quickly put away the papers in one of the packed bags and ran to help his beautiful pregnant wife. He put his hands on Mary's hips, lifted her up, and sat her down on their trusted companion. She sat with her legs to one side of the animal, her hands gripping the reins. She leaned over to put her cheek against the back of the donkey's mane and closed her eyes.

"Please be strong and take us to Bethlehem safely, sweet girl," Mary whispered to the donkey as she rubbed the underside of the animal's neck.

"Who's talking to the donkey now?" Joseph said. Now he smirked back.

"Oh, hush!" Mary said, swatting the air and sitting back up.

"Lord God, please give us strength and safe passage to Bethlehem," Mary continued, looking up at the fading stars.

"Amen," Joseph said. "And thank you for my beautiful wife."

"A-men!" Mary responded with a huge smile.

The sun was just about to peek over the distant mountains as Mary, Joseph, and the donkey started on their way out of Nazareth, and on the long road to Bethlehem.

Back in Heaven, Gabriel was watching over Mary and Joseph through the Eye. "It never ceases to amaze me what God can do," he said to himself. Then, turning his gaze upward, he said, "God, I am ready for more. What would You like me to do next?"

The wind blew. The same force Mary felt in the garden, Gabriel could also feel, for God is the creator of Heaven *and* Earth.

"Gabriel, you have done well!" His words rumbled across the hills. **"And yes, there is more work to be done!"**

"I am ready, Lord," Gabriel responded.

"You see, Mary and Joseph, Elizabeth and Zechariah, Caesar Augustus, all his soldiers, and even the donkey Mary is riding are part of this plan. Now we need to prepare for Jesus to come into the world.

My Son is the King of kings, but will have the heart of a shepherd, to usher in My people to be closer to Me as I promised so many years ago."

"What else can I do, Master?"

"You must do three things:

First, there are three noblemen from the East traveling in the desert. Go tell these men I am delivering the promised Messiah, and they are to welcome Him.

Second, you must convince a humble young shepherd to come witness Jesus' birth.

And finally, Jesus must be born at the inn on the far side of Bethlehem. Prepare a spectacular celebration for Him.

Go, be the light. Show them the way."

EXODUS 23:20

"See, I am sending an angel ahead of you to guard you along the way and to bring you to the place I have prepared."

DECEMBER 14
A Light in the Sky

God's command was simple, but Gabriel knew how important his new tasks were. First, he needed to find the three noblemen in the desert. He had to think of a different way to approach them, a more face-to-face interaction to get their attention. Grabbing a tattered scarf and a worn robe, he imitated the look of a fellow tired traveler. His traveled appearance would be a way for him to get close to the men without causing suspicion.

He was ready. The sky above Gabriel once again began to swirl, opening to reveal the Eye of Heaven. He jumped into the hurricane of light and began his journey deep into the dunes of the Eastern desert.

With a bright flash, Gabriel instantly found his feet sinking into the earth beneath him. The environment was much different than he was used to in Heaven. It was hot, windy, and dry. Not much for plant life except for a few mangled acacia trees and spots of saltbrush. Everything else was piles of fine dirt and rock. Gabriel took a few steps. Sand was already in his sandals and getting into his human-form eyes. This didn't bother him though; he was there for a purpose.

The late sun hung low in the western sky. Long shadows stretched across the rolling hills of powdered earth that rippled like an ocean. The heat of the day was still present, but the cool of the night hovered above, waiting to settle in. Gabriel walked on.

The sun finally slipped behind the distant horizon, and a flicker of light caught Gabriel's eye. He continued walking to see what it was. As he got closer, he could see four large tents centered around a fire—it was a camp. Three men dressed in fine clothes sat around the fire,

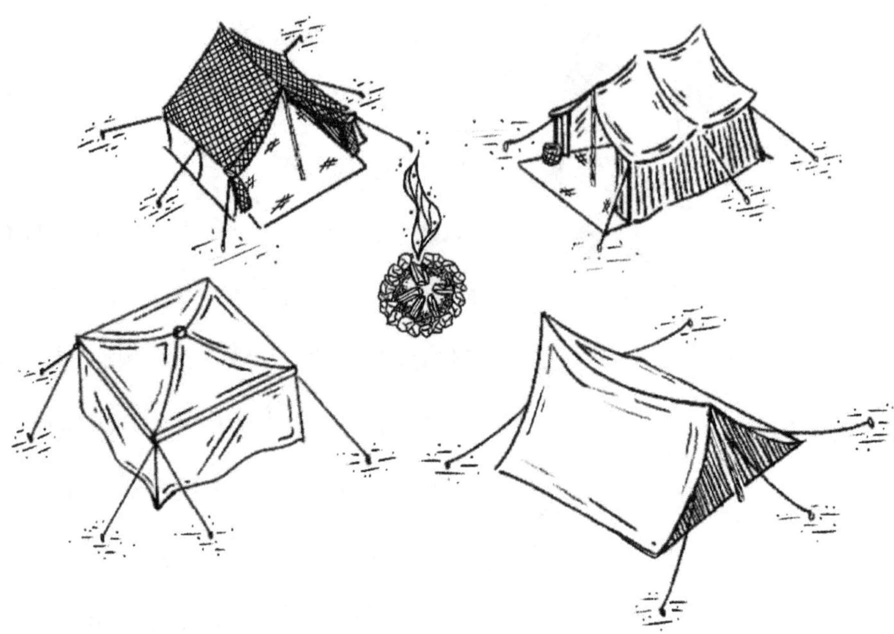

laughing and eating while a small group of other men, who appeared to be helpers, prepared beds, made more food, and tended to their camels. Gabriel was confident these were the men God told him to find.

The disguised angel approached slowly, like he had traveled from a long distance—he had, not from a neighboring town, but all the way from Heaven! One of the well-dressed men noticed Gabriel and yelled out, "Hello, fellow traveler!" His voice was excited and merry. "You look as though you have walked the entire desert; please, come join us. We have food and drink to share." He held his arms out wide with a golden chalice in one hand, welcoming Gabriel to join them.

"That is very kind of you. Thank you, sir." Gabriel replied, walking over to the men, finally able to see them more clearly in the fire's light.

"Come, sit... I am Caspar," the man introduced himself. His head was covered by a white turban with a large red ruby centered above his forehead. A blue robe traced with white silk and a cloak embroidered with pearls that looked like a map of the stars hung from his shoulders, fastened across his chest by a golden chain. "What's your name, young lad?"

"I am Gabriel," he said with an angelic smile. "I am a messenger looking for some people, and I guess I've stumbled upon your camp." He said everything except that it was them who he was looking for.

Counter to Gabriel's desire, Caspar had a feeling this was no ordinary traveler. He squinted at Gabriel and asked, "Are you hungry? We have lots of food to share."

Gabriel nodded. His earthly stomach was hollow, rolling around in his body, and growling like a wild beast. Although food on earth wasn't just a necessity, it *was* a fun treat.

One of the helpers passed by, and Caspar kindly asked him to bring Gabriel some food, water, and a change of clothes.

The other two men, also dressed in luxurious clothing, introduced themselves. There was Balthazar, a tall man made even taller by the crown he wore. His skin was the color of cocoa and he had a bright smile that matched his robe. The third was Melchior, older than the rest, whose gray beard contrasted with the royal green and gold cloth draped over his shoulders. Atop his head was a tall, pointy hat embroidered with colorful jewels and gems.

Moments later, the helper returned with the items Caspar had requested for their guest. Gabriel ate and drank a modest portion and tried to participate in the conversation around the fire. They loved their fine clothes, their abundance of food, and talking about how smart they were—these were worldly men.

What about giving thanks and praise to God for all of these blessings? Gabriel asked himself. *Am I with the right group?* He thought, second-guessing his company.

"Yes, Gabriel, be bold. Deliver them to Me and bring them to Jesus. All are welcome," God flooded his mind.

Gabriel thought for a moment more. How could he get the three noblemen to travel to Bethlehem? Then it came to him. He looked up from staring into the fire and said to the men, "You all seem to be very smart. Do you also know a lot about the stars?"

The three men looked at Gabriel, proud of themselves.

"We have studied and know *all* about the stars." Melchior's nose lifted into the sky. "Some would say we are astrologers."

"Great! Maybe you can help me then." Gabriel pushed his eyebrows as high as they could go. "While I was out roaming the desert, I noticed a star I have never seen before. Can you tell me anything about it?"

"Of course we can help," Melchior's voice still filled with arrogant undertones. "Point us to the star and we will be able to tell you everything you want to know about it."

Gabriel took a moment to scan the speckled night sky. He extended his hand toward the distant mountains, which were in the direction of Bethlehem.

"There!" Gabriel pointed. In that moment, a bright star appeared in the sky. "To the west, between the peaks of the mountains."

Melchior didn't say a word, but Balthazar stood and stared out toward the mountains, shielding his eyes from the glare of the fire. "We have been out here for weeks and we have not seen this," he said in amazement.

It was a star, a dazzling gem in the night sky flickering between the brightest whites and spectacular shades of purple and blue.

"I've been calling it the King Star." Gabriel added, "looks like a crown sitting on top of the mountains."

Then Melchior and Caspar both stood up to join Balthazar. The three men were drawn away from the fire and into the dark to get a better look. Unable to break their gaze, Caspar said, "It is certainly beautiful. Like no other star I've ever seen before."

The desert night stretched endlessly, the only movement was the gentle flickering of the fire and the shifting sand beneath the rolling wind. The three men stood in silent awe, their gaze locked on the light hanging above the distant mountains. They would soon real-ize it wasn't just a star, but an invitation.

MATTHEW 2:10

"When they saw the star, they were overjoyed."

DECEMBER 15
The Dream of a Noble Man

The star had appeared so suddenly, so brilliantly. It was as if Gabriel himself had painted it into existence. Its light cut through the darkness and was unlike any other star the three men had studied before. But even in their wonder, Balthazar turned to notice that Gabriel was no longer with them. "Where did our little friend go?" he asked the others.

"He was just here," Melchior said, scanning the camp's edge, beyond the tents, where the firelight faded into darkness.

"It's as if he just vanished," Caspar responded, starting to realize Gabriel was no ordinary person. He had come with a purpose, to lead them to this very moment. And now, he was gone. "There is something special about that boy and that star. We should travel to those western mountains at first light." The others nodded in agreement, and with their minds made up, they each retired to their tents to get some sleep.

Each of the men had their own bedtime routine, but they all had some combination of washing up, brushing teeth, and putting on pajamas. After some time, the glow from the lanterns of each tent fell dim, signifying sleep was near. They were ready for rest, they had a big day of travel ahead of them.

Simultaneously, the three men laid on their mats, closed their eyes...

and began...

to dream...

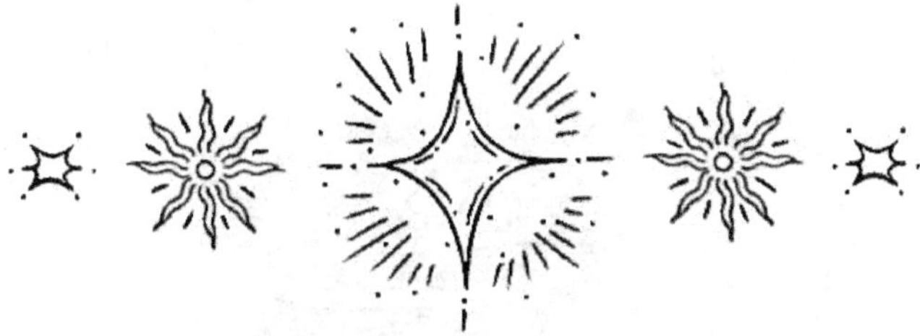

It was as if they had been lifted from their bodies and were drawn beyond the natural world. The desert melted away like the top of an hourglass sinking to the bottom. In its place, a dark sky stretched endlessly, filled with the glow of a single, blazing star.

But it wasn't just a star—it was Gabriel! He shimmered like a guiding light. His face was sincere, but his eyes were filled with urgency.

Below him, nestled between some rolling hills, was a small town. A town they recognized and would have typically journeyed past. It was the town of Bethlehem.

Gabriel lifted a hand and pointed downward. There, bathed in the glow of Gabriel's light, was a newborn child. He lay in a crib made of rough wood and lined with hay. Nailed to the side was an inscription, the letters carved with divine purpose.

Resting on the baby's tiny head sat a crown, not of gold, not of jewels, but of the glory and power of God.

Gabriel's voice rang out, "Come, follow me, and welcome Him."

As they gazed at the child, Gabriel began to shine brighter and brighter, until his very presence dissolved into the light of the great star above.

The morning sun filled the tents. The men bolted upright, their breath was fast and their hearts pounded through their clothes, unaware of their shared dream.

JEREMIAH 10:7

"Who should not fear you, King of the nations? This is your due. Among all the wise leaders of the nations and in all their kingdoms, there is no one like you."

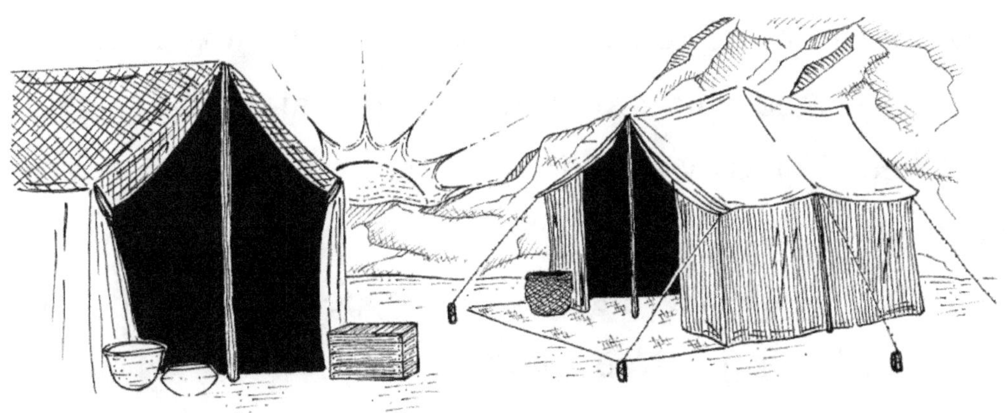

DECEMBER 16
A Shared Dream Revealed

The camp was silent. The helpers of the three men exchanged puzzled glances as they waited for their leaders to wake. The camp had been packed up, except for the three tents where the men still lay asleep. *First light* meant before sunrise, but the sun had already risen above the horizon and the heat had its grip on the day.

At last, the men emerged from their tents. They were still in sync with each other and yet still unaware. The helpers scrambled to pack up the rest of the camp as the men converged where the camels were waiting.

"Well, I guess we didn't get the early start we were hoping for," Caspar joked. "You guys overslept."

"WE overslept?" Balthazar snapped back. "I was waiting to hear from you two."

"Oh, give it up. We all slept in," Melchior said, cutting through the nonsense. "Let's just get packed up and head west like we agreed last night."

Just before mid-morning, they finally stepped off toward the western mountains. The caravan moved quietly without Caspar's usual commentary, or Melchior's arrogant philosophies, or Balthazar's witty comebacks. Only the rhythmic steps of the camels' broad feet and the soft jingle of the metal clasps on their harnesses relieved the awkward quiet. The three men were lost in thought, uncertain of what to make of the dream they had.

Caspar couldn't take the silence any longer. He cleared his throat, turned to Melchior, who was deep in his own thoughts, and said, "That young lad who came to our camp told us about the star, and then vanished. Then that very same boy was in a dream I had last night. He was talking about a king being born in Bethlehem, but the vision was unlike anything I have ever seen before. What do you make of this?"

Melchior turned his head slowly to look at Caspar. His face was pale. "You saw it too?" Melchior confessed.

"*Too*? What do you mean, *too*?" Caspar repeated himself. He was caught off guard.

Just then, Balthazar guided his camel closer, his expression tense. "So did I."

The three men looked at one another, their silence now charged with wonder and excitement.

"How is this even possible?" Melchior questioned. His academics were being challenged by the supernatural.

This all but confirmed Casper's suspicion. "I believe that young man was an angel of God," Caspar answered. "He was sent to us for this very reason!"

"Now Caspar, you are a man of science. We look to the stars for signs and books for knowledge. We are wise men." Melchior responded, refusing to surrender his pride.

"Yes, but what greater sign than a beautiful star for us to seek? If it is a book you need, it was written in the Jewish book of Isaiah that the Lord Himself would give us a sign. And here it is."

"Perhaps," Melchior conceded. "We will see," he shrugged with uncertainty.

"So, let's go to Bethlehem!" Caspar said excitedly.

"Sure, but you do realize to reach Bethlehem we will be in King Herod's land?" Melchior said, hoping this might change his companions' minds. King Herod ruled over the land and no foreign dignitary would dare cross into it without first seeking an audience with him.

"You're right. It would be seen as an insult if we didn't stop," Caspar noted grimly.

"Herod is... unpredictable," Balthazar murmured. "But we cannot ignore him."

"Well then, we must first go to Jerusalem to meet with Herod," Caspar directed. "On to Bethlehem."

Though uneasy about their meeting with King Herod, the dream had stirred something within them that was greater than fear. The call to seek out the newborn King was undeniable and nothing, not even Herod, would keep them from uncovering the truth.

ISAIAH 7:14

"Therefore the Lord himself will give you a sign: The virgin will conceive and give birth to a son, and will call him Immanuel."

DECEMBER 17
King Herod

Melchior, Caspar, and Balthazar rode in silence as they approached the city of Jerusalem. The great stone wall seemed to grow taller with every step toward the city, intimidating as both a physical barrier and a symbol of power and might. The camels' feet pressed into the stone-paved road leading to the city's massive gates. The gates were so large, their three camels could walk side-by-side through the opening and still have enough room on either side for their helpers. When closed, the space was not blocked by just any piece of wood, but what seemed like whole trunks of trees, reinforced with iron brackets and steel rods.

On this day, the great gates stood open. It was not an invitation to enter, it was a mandatory checkpoint. Armed guards stood watch and checked every traveler who intended to pass through.

As the caravan moved closer, their presence drew a lot of attention. The people outside of the gate started to crowd around to get a glimpse of the lavish men. Many royal families and noblemen had visited before but three

at once was rare. A few of Herod's soldiers, stationed near the gate, quickly took notice and approached them.

"Who are you, and what business do you bring to Jerusalem?" one of the guards demanded, his grip firm on the hilt of his sword.

Melchior looked at the man respectfully and said, "We are lords from the Eastern kingdoms, here to pay our respects to King Herod before continuing on our journey."

The guards exchanged glances with each other, then motioned for them to follow. "The king will decide if he wishes to see you," the soldier barked back.

They were led through the bustling streets of Jerusalem. People, animals, carts, all filled the streets, just enough room to pass by single-file. Merchants lined the road selling their wares and others selling food. The lively crowd rumbled, a symphony of indistinct voices. The sound echoed off the old clay buildings—beige and brown, all seamless to each other, making it impossible to distinguish where one building ended and the next began.

The group walked to the center of the city. There it was, the royal palace. A grand structure that stood apart from the rest. It looked as though it was carved of a single mountain of pure, white marble. Another wall surrounded the estate. Evenly spaced stone pillars anchored to the ground while black iron scrolls curled and stretched to join them together, leaving space for the common people to view the royal residence. Specially trained palace soldiers manned the gates and patrolled the grounds.

Upon reaching the entrance, the three noblemen dismounted their camels and left them in the care of their helpers. They were ushered across the courtyard and up the swooping staircase to the grand entry. The cool interior of the palace was lined with massive columns, the floors smooth and polished, as expected with Roman-style architecture. More soldiers waited at the end of the long hallway. They were positioned on either side of the large wooden door to the throne room, their faces expression-less.

From the other side of the door, the three men could hear a herald bang his staff against the hard marble floor, his voice loud but muffled through the thick cedar planks. "The lords from the East seek an audience with his Majesty, King Herod!"

The huge wooden doors swung open. The dull murmurs of the room's occupants were hushed by the sound of the hinges wrenching under the pressure of the heavy wood and iron. The three men stepped inside, shoulder-to-shoulder.

Many people filled the room. Some appeared as though reveling with the king was a permanent occupation. At the far end of the chamber, King Herod lounged on his golden throne. He was a large man with a heavy brow and a scowl permanently etched upon his face. Draped in fine robes, he reclined with a young servant girl standing beside him, holding a golden platter of figs and honeyed dates to snack on.

At their entrance, he barely moved, unamused by his uninvited guests.

"What brings you to my kingdom, oh great *'lords of the Eastern kingdoms'*?" Herod's voice spewed with mockery across the chasm between them.

Caspar took a step forward and bowed. "We have come to pay our respects to you, Your Majesty. We are traveling through your land to follow a star, one that heralds the birth of a great king. We seek the child who is to be born on your land."

Herod's hand, which had been reaching lazily for another piece of fruit, froze midair. His jaw tightened and his eyes narrowed. *A king? A child?* His mind churned. He had spent years eliminating any threats to his throne, and now *this*?

He forced a smile and raised himself up, now interested in what the three men were saying. "A king, you say? This is most... interesting. I too wish to know more about this, *baby king.*" His voice was smooth, but his eyes were full of darkness. "Let me send my men to accompany you. Together, we shall find this king and welcome him accordingly."

Balthazar interrupted, bowing slightly. "That is most generous, Your Majesty, but we wouldn't wish to burden you. We don't know the exact location of this child. It was brought to us in a dream."

The king leaned back and burst out in a hysterical laugh. Others in the room joined in. "A dream?" The king paused to laugh more. "You are in search of a baby king... from a dream? I thought you'd be more rational than that, being *noble* and, *wise men.*"

Melchior stepped forward, the crowd still laughing, he forced an uneasy laugh of his own. "It is a foolish notion," he stated, dismissing its divine significance, "but if it pleases the king, we shall continue our journey to seek the truth." A pit opened in his heart, a feeling of emptiness, like he said something wrong. His mind went silent, except for a bold and pure voice, **"Come, follow the light."**

"Very well," Herod agreed. "But you must return and tell me where to find this baby king, so that I too can visit and pay homage."

The three men nodded their heads in agreement, though they knew they would do no such thing. If the dream was true, Herod would order the baby to be killed. If the dream was just a dream, they would be mocked and laughed at again.

Herod, still reeling from the laughter, invited the three men to stay for dinner. He clapped his hands, a gesture that started a procession of servants carrying more golden trays filled with an abundance of food. Roasted lamb, spiced lentils, fresh dates, olives, fresh bread—too much to eat. Wine was poured into jeweled goblets and the whole room burst into merry excitement.

"Let us feast in your honor," Herod declared, motioning to his visitors, but no attention was given to them. It was an empty tribute.

Melchior, Balthazar, and Caspar ate sparingly. They had no appetite. A feeling of belittlement filled their stomachs instead, nor did they wish to linger longer than necessary.

At last, the three men found an opportunity to leave when King Herod was distracted by the entertainment of a juggler in mid act. They quickly walked through the palace halls where during the day it seemed beautiful and grand, but at night it felt like a cave, cold and dark. The noble men went to the back exit where they knew their camels and trusted helpers would be waiting. They reached the doors that separated them from freedom, and the guardsmen standing there let them out.

Behind them, the doors closed and they stepped onto the dirt path leading to the stables. Though the sound of a great feast continued from inside, they were relieved to be free of Herod's oppressive rule.

Looking up, Melchior saw the star. It was bigger and brighter than before. There was something different, more pronounced about that star and the sky around it was dancing.

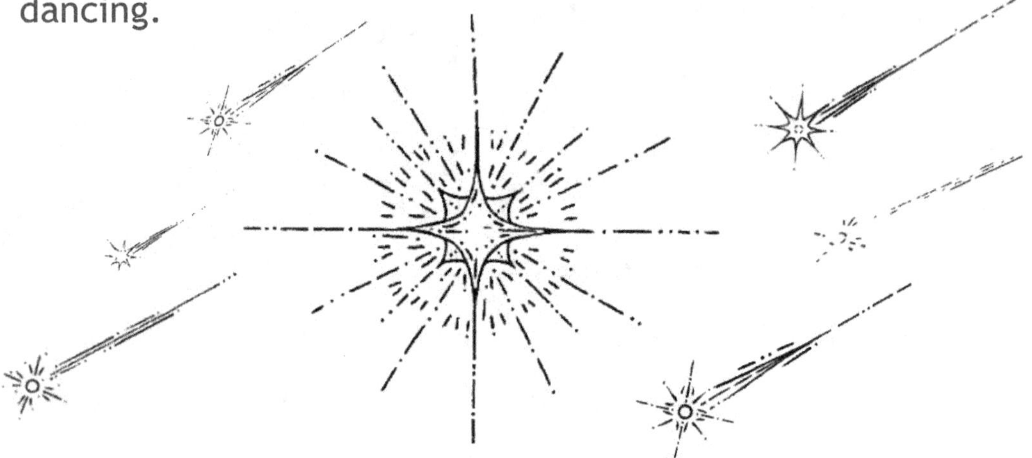

"We go tonight," he declared. "Bethlehem is only a few hours away. I must know."

Their helpers prepared the camels and pulled them along in tow. They marched back through the now quiet streets and left Jerusalem with the star as their guiding light.

PROVERBS 23:1 & 3

"1 When you sit to dine with a ruler,

note well what is before you,

3 Do not crave his delicacies,

for that food is deceptive."

DECEMBER 18
Shepherd of Men

High in the cool mountains above Bethlehem, a young shepherd named Joshua, rested along a quiet trail. His head lay on a large rock and his side on the ground. Light from the morning sun warmed his face, relaxing him after a cold morning of chores.

Joshua had been up since before dawn, rounding up the sheep, guiding them to food, and keeping a watchful eye for dangerous animals. He wasn't the most experienced shepherd but he was good. With all his flock accounted for and safely grazing, he allowed himself a moment to rest. The wind swept through the rugged terrain, rustling the sparse patches of grass around him and carrying the sound of his sheep bleating across the hills. His eyelids grew heavy as he drifted into a deep sleep.

And then...

he began...

to dream...

The voice of an angel called out to him. "It's hard work being a shepherd, but now is no time to rest. You are missing One."

Joshua's heart nearly pounded out of his chest. The beat was like a mallet against a drum. Missing one? That can't be. He had counted them all!

Oh, where could my little one be? He thought. *I know I had all my sheep when I started.*

Frantic, he began searching.

Maybe the lost sheep had wandered around the mountain? Or crossed the river? Perhaps it hid behind the trees? But no matter how far he searched, he could not find it.

His chest tightened. *Oh Lord, please help me find this sheep. My father will be so unhappy if I have lost one.*

Then, the voice returned, "You have not lost a sheep. You are missing the Lamb of God in your life."

Joshua froze, his breath caught in wonder.

"Through a young woman from Nazareth, a baby boy will be sent to this Earth as a sacrifice. He will bear the weight of the world's sin and will make those who follow Him pure so they can enter the kingdom of God. When the time is right, He will become the Shepherd of Man, and you will be welcomed into His flock. He will take care of all who believe in Him, just as you care for and love your sheep. Now, wake!"

A gust of wind swirled around him, and the dream dissolved into light.

Joshua's eyes slowly opened. The hills were unchanged, but something felt different, like they carried new life.

Then, the sound of footsteps crunching on the path caught his attention. Another traveler was walking toward him. Joshua could tell the traveler was young with a small frame, but he was unable to see their face because the sun sat perfectly behind them, casting a dark silhouette.

Joshua didn't feel threatened, but more curious. He raised a hand to try to see into the light, but it didn't help. Their steps were direct and purposeful, straight toward the resting shepherd. They stopped at his feet.

The person hung over Joshua and said, "It's hard work being a shepherd."

MATTHEW 18:12

"What do you think? If a man owns a hundred sheep, and one of them wanders away, will he not leave the ninety-nine on the hills and go to look for the one that wandered off?"

DECEMBER 19
Shepherd Him In

"It's hard work being a shepherd," said the traveler to Joshua.

Joshua's breath escaped his body. The words from his dream echoed in his mind. 

"Why yes, it is," Joshua replied with a confused hesitation. "Who are you?"

"Name's Gabriel," the angelic young voice said, bracing his hands to catch himself as he sat down next to Joshua.

Joshua stared at Gabriel, now able to clearly see his face. Gabriel's milky skin contrasted with his brown tussled hair, his blue eyes, and his soft smile. *Who is this? And why did his presence feel so familiar, so... holy?* he wondered.

"Do you believe God can do anything?" Gabriel continued.

Joshua's chest fluttered with excitement. He loved God above everything else, even his sheep.

"Of course!" Joshua replied.

Gabriel lit up with joy. "I am an angel of God. He sent me to deliver a message to you; He is sending His only Son to Earth, to be born to a sweet, innocent girl. He is the promised Messiah and will take on all the sins of those who believe in Him as their Lord and Savior."

"This is amazing! The One we have been waiting for, the *One* from my dream!" Joshua's voice rose with excitement. "But why are you telling *me*?"

"You have proven yourself faithful, kind, and obedient, so God asked me to invite you to come and welcome His Son, whose birth will be tonight. A bright light will hang over the town and you will hear songs of praise. Come down the mountain and meet Him."

The most electrifying sense of joy surged through Joshua, so intense that he could barely contain it. "The Messiah is coming?" he gasped. "To Bethlehem? And I get to witness it?"

He had heard the prophecies spoken by the elders in town about the One they had been waiting for, the Messiah, and now the time had come!

Gabriel smiled. "Yes, yes, and yes. He will be born in the city of David. Just as it is written."

Joshua's heart was bursting with excitement. He had to tell someone! His parents, his friends, everyone in Bethlehem needed to hear this!

He leaped off the ground, and raised his hands to heaven. "God, You are so good. Thank you for choosing me to be a part of Your Son's coming!" Tears rolled down his cheeks. A humble shepherd boy, unseen by most, was being rewarded by God Himself.

Then Joshua turned back toward Gabriel, still sitting on the ground. "Thank you, Gabriel! I hope to see you again."

"I think you will," he said, smiling back and winking.

Joshua turned and started running home to tell his parents.

Gabriel could hear the boy's joyful laugh and words of praise fade as he got further down the path.

"What a good kid," Gabriel said to himself. Then the sound of bleating sheep came into focus. In the boy's excitement, the young shepherd forgot his sheep. "Well, I guess I will herd this flock home?"

LUKE 2:15

"When the angels had left them and gone into heaven, the shepherds said to one another, 'Let's go to Bethlehem and see this thing that has happened, which the Lord has told us about.'"

DECEMBER 20
An Innkeeper's Prayer

A few months earlier, news of the census started to spread across the land. People even gave it the nickname 'The Count'. But everyone wondered why Caesar Augustus even wanted one. Some thought it was a plan to expand the city. Others were hoping Caesar would split King Herod's kingdom. And yet others knew it was for a more predictable reason...

"They're going to raise our taxes. I just know it," said Elias, a humble innkeeper in Bethlehem, to his wife, Miriam. "What are we going to do? We can't even pay the bills we already owe, let alone more taxes."

"God will find a way for us," she said, trying to put her husband's worries at ease.

Elias began to pray, "Great and all-powerful, God. I come before you to humbly ask that you save us, we need help!" His trust was in God, but he didn't know how to get the money.

Their inn was at the far end of town, hidden from most visitors. Other places were closer to the main road and easier to get to. So, with the lack of guests and little money coming in, their inn had fallen into disrepair.

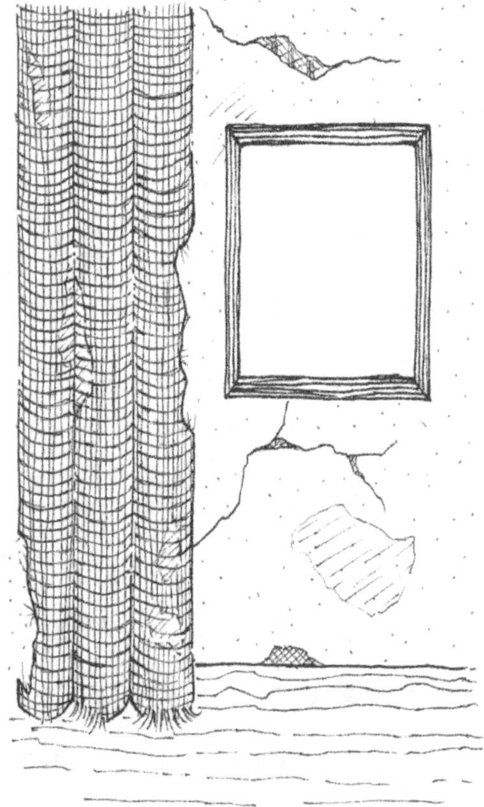

Paint had chipped off the walls, beds were broken, curtains were torn, and doors were falling off their hinges. People were not interested in staying there.

Then one day, while Elias and Miriam were tidying up the welcome room off the entry, a boy walked through their door looking for work.

"I would like a job!" he said. No hello nor introduction, just straight to business. "I am pretty handy and I can help fix this place up."

Elias looked to see a young boy ready to work, a tool bag in either hand and a smile on his face. He replied with a laugh and said, "You are far too young to get a job. Run along and go play." The innkeeper's hand waved in the air to dismiss the young maintenance boy.

"I may look young, but I am older than you think," he responded back. "My Father sent me to come here and help you restore your beautiful inn."

"This *was* once a beautiful inn," Elias's face fell, disappointed he let his business go into such a poor state. He was about to ask the young repairman about his father but a momentary pause left room for the boy to respond instead.

"I can certainly see that," he said joyfully. "This place is a gift from God and he would like you to make it great again. And I would like to help."

"You know what? You are absolutely right. God is a creator, and He didn't stop until His creation was perfect, so I should not give up either." Elias's hopes were raised until he looked at his empty cash register. "But I cannot pay you a fair wage."

"That's no problem. I am happy to work for a meal and a place to stay."

"What is your name, young lad?" Elias asked with his spirits cautiously raised.

"My name is Gabriel," he said with a twinkle in his eye.

"Well alright then, Gabriel. Let's get to work!" A long smile spread across the innkeeper's face as he looked over at his wife. Miriam responded with a relieved smile of her own.

The three worked as one, cleaning, repairing, and making everything anew. Miriam was excellent at cleaning, Gabriel could fix anything, and Elias was a craftsman, he loved to build with his hands. They all had their gifts to share.

At the end of each day, they would all sit by the hearth in the welcome room, eating simple meals and sharing stories. Elias noticed Gabriel never asked for much. Though there were now good, clean rooms available, Gabriel would still choose to sleep in the stable out back, lying on the hay.

"You don't have to sleep out there, you know," Elias told him one night. "There's a soft bed inside."

Gabriel simply smiled. "It's actually pretty comfortable, I sleep like a baby out there."

Elias chuckled. "You're an odd kid, Gabriel."

Months passed, and at last, the inn was back to new. Beds were made, the roof no longer leaked, and the  walls stood strong. It was a welcoming place again, ready for travelers and just in time for the census.

The three of them stood outside, now almost like a family, looking at all they had done.

Elias held out his arms reaching for both Miriam and Gabriel's hands. He started to pray, "Almighty Creator of Heaven and Earth, we have put in the work. We now give it to You, to bring the people to stay with us. Please guide us and use us to do Your will. Amen." Then he turned to Gabriel, "Thank you so much. We couldn't have done this without you."

Gabriel responded sincerely, "All the Glory to God! I was happy to help."

The next morning, Gabriel was gone. No footprints in the dust, no belongings left behind, only the work of his hands remained. Elias searched the town, but no one had seen him leave.

1 THESSALONIANS 5:16-18

"16 Rejoice always, 17 pray continually, 18 give thanks in all circumstances; for this is God's will for you in Christ Jesus."

DECEMBER 21
Hope Restored

The census was drawing people to Bethlehem. The little town was about to get a big wave of visitors, but Elias and Miriam's inn was located on the far side of the town. So when the people started to arrive, the other inns, closer to the main road, filled up first. Officially, the census was a couple of days away, but time was running out and their rooms still sat completely empty. All the work and all the preparation to restore their inn may have been for nothing. A full inn was their last hope to stay in business.

The sun had fallen and rose again—now it was the day before the great Roman census. If they were to get visitors, this would need to be the day. Elias's mind was filled with thoughts of failure and disappointment.

"Don't lose hope, God is with us," Miriam said when she saw her husband. She could tell he was worried. After decades of marriage, she could pick up on these things. "I tell you what, I'm going to the market to buy a large roast for dinner tonight, for *all* our guests." The word 'all' made her head nod.

"We don't have the money for that, love." Elias responded.

"I will go and see what I can find." Her mind was set. She walked over to get a headscarf and her coin purse from behind the counter. As she picked up the leather pouch meant to hold money, there was but a single coin. The dance of multiple coins singing a jolly jingle was but a silent solo. She barely had enough to buy a bundle of wheat, let alone a whole roast. This didn't discourage her though. "God will provide," she said to Elias as she walked out of the door.

Miriam had a forty-minute walk to the market but she could already tell the downtown streets were bustling with activity. Even at this distance, a low murmur echoed between the alleyways, and she could see a plume of dust hover over the distant market. The scarf she grabbed as she was leaving would come in handy to cover her head and her face as she got closer.

At first, Miriam was walking the street alone. But as she got closer, more and more people joined her. With every step, the dirt that was once compacted into a road was ground into a fine dust that lifted into the air. As expected, Miriam pulled the tail of her scarf across her face so she wouldn't breathe it in. The market was just around the next block and she could hear the roar of voices coming from the other side of the building like an awakening beast. She turned the corner and there it was—the market.

Her quiet town of Bethlehem was filled to bursting. There were so many people walking through the market— visitors from other places and vendors she had never seen before. The vendors were just here to take advantage of the growing crowd. Miriam cautiously stepped into the flow of people. She felt as though she might be taken by a riptide out to sea.

Then her attention shifted, away from the people, to a weeping boy. She heard his cry above everything else. Tears ran down his face. He was scared and alone, crying out for his mother.

"Moooommmyyyyyyy!" Bubbles formed on his lips when they touched.

Miriam pulled her scarf down off of her face and ran over to the boy, trying not to scare him. She knelt down in front of the crying child and placed her hands on his shoulder, looking him in the eyes. He didn't look like a stray, he was well dressed, and as clean as any boy his age could be.

"Are you lost?" She asked the boy. Her voice was pitched higher than normal but calming for the boy.

He sniffled and nodded, relieved that someone stopped to help.

"What's your name, sweetheart?"

"Toby." His little voice was shaky and raw.

Miriam smiled at Toby. He looked pitiful, but he was cute.

"I'm Miriam. Can I sit with you?"

Again, he nodded his head.

Before she sat down, she noticed a baker selling fresh bread just across from where they were. The smell of sourdough always brings a smile to her face. Her mouth started to water with the thought of sharing a loaf with the boy.

"Wait here one moment, I will be right back." She said to the boy. "I am just going across the street to get a little snack for us."

Miriam rushed across the dirt and stone road over to the baker's cart. She pulled open her purse and pulled out her last coin. She looked at the small piece of metal and then the baker, "What can I buy with this?" Her face winced, hoping there was something.

The man looked at her and said apologetically, "I am sorry, I don't have anything for that price." His head moved from side-to-side and with a sympathy smile.

Miriam's face fell. She looked back at the boy staring back at her. She turned back to the baker and pleaded with him, "Please, even just a slice?"

The man's smile transformed from sympathetic to compassionate. "Okay, I will do that." He reached down into a basket and pulled out a round loaf. With both hands he tore a piece off and handed it to Miriam. The outer shell was crispy, flakes burst in the air releasing the scent of baked yeast into her nose. It wasn't a large piece, but it would certainly satisfy the boy.

She handed the baker her last coin and walked back to Toby. He didn't move an inch from when Miriam left. Remnants of the boy's tears still etched down his cheek like a dried up stream of mud—it made Miriam laugh.

The two sat down on the ground and chatted with each other. Miriam did most of the talking while the boy enjoyed his piece of bread. Then she heard a woman call out, then a man, "Tobias! Tobias!"

"Over here!" Miriam waved her hand at the frantic couple. She hopped off the dirty ground, straightened out her dress, and said, "I found him here all alone. I hope it's okay, I bought him a slice of bread from the baker."

The mother ran over and scooped up the boy into her arms, still reeling from the panic. Then she put him down and stared into her son's eyes, finally she was able to say, "Thank God you are okay. I thought we lost you." Words of worry left her mouth, but a breath of relief came flowing in. Both Toby's parents continued to hug the little boy, embracing each other as a family.

After some time, the dad stood up and looked at Miriam with gratitude, "Thank you *so* much! I wish we could pay you for watching our son, but we don't have enough money to give. We just got into town with our group, and we're finding the inns here are either too expensive or there are simply no more rooms available. We are hopeful we'll find something, but when we do, we'll need every bit of money to stay."

Miriam's eyes broke away from the man's and looked to Heaven. She smiled, shook her head in disbelief and said, "God, *You* are so good!" Then she looked back at the man and his family, "You owe me nothing, but my husband and I own an inn up the street. We have plenty of beds and we will not charge you an expensive rate. I invite you and your entire group to stay with us."

Miriam and Toby led the way like grand marshals in a parade. At least one hundred people with carts and animals of all kinds walked with them to the far side of Bethlehem.

Elias was sitting and saw Miriam lead the large group right up to the entrance. She and the rest started filing into the welcome room. One-by-one, the room was packed to bursting.

"How did you...? What did you...? Where did you...?" Elias was in shock, unable to find the right question to ask.

"I believe the right question you are looking for is, 'Who did this?' and the answer is God!" Miriam said with a humble smile.

They began to check people in—it took hours. In the end, every room was occupied and the stable was full of animals. They even set up mats in the welcome room as overflow.

Their inn had new life and people liked the fresh look. Some said they remembered it being in disrepair but now they were pleasantly surprised at the transformation. They said it was beautiful and that they would love to come back. Elias and Miriam were finally able to offer a clean, safe place for their visitors to stay.

"My love, God is so good. He heard our prayer." Elias said to his wife. "Thank you for going to the market and having the faith that this would all work out."

Miriam replied with joy in every word. "With God, all things are possible."

The door opened a few times after this with late arriving travelers looking for a place to stay, but Elias was now turning them away. "I'm sorry, we have no more space." His joy was met with guilt. He cared for all his visitors and didn't want to turn anyone away.

Miriam touched Elias's arm, looked up to her husband and said, "I don't like turning them away."

"I know," Elias responded. "But what more can we do?"

Then, the door swung open once more. A man stumbled inside, his face lined with exhaustion. His clothes were dusty from the road, and his shoulders slumped from the weight of travel.

"Please," he said, his voice raw. "My wife is pregnant and we need a place to stay."

Elias and Miriam exchanged a look, and now his guilt turned to anguish; there was no room, not in the house, not even on the floor. "I am so sorry, friend, we have no room. We are filled to bursting."

"Please, we will take anything. We have been traveling for days, it's late, and there are no more rooms anywhere in Bethlehem. I can't have my pregnant wife sleeping on the street." The man's voice pleaded for a miracle.

Then Elias thought of Gabriel, the young helper who had worked for them in exchange for a place to stay and a meal. He had slept in the stable and said it was very comfortable.

Elias sighed and put a hand on the man's shoulder. "We have nothing left inside, and I know it's not much, but we had a helper sleep out in our stable. He said it was a great place to sleep. You are welcome to stay there. It's dry, there's fresh hay, and it's away from the street."

"That will be just fine. Thank you," the man said, relieved he and his wife were finally going to get some rest.

PSALM 9:1-2

"¹ I will give thanks to you, Lord, with all my heart;
I will tell of all your wonderful deeds.
² I will be glad and rejoice in you;
I will sing the praises of your name, O Most High."

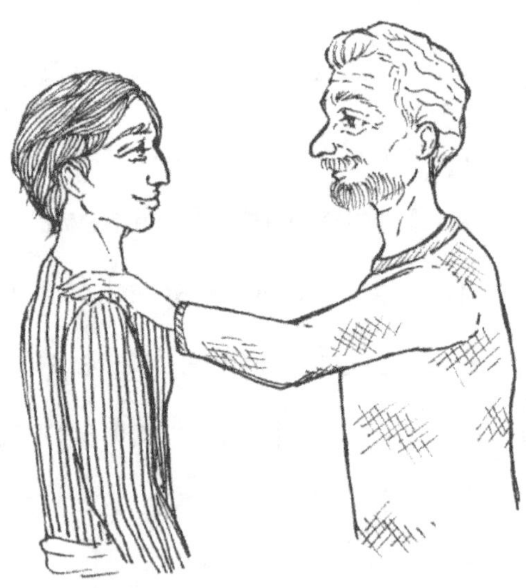

DECEMBER 22
The Arrival

It took over a week to travel through the desert from Nazareth to Bethlehem, but finally Mary and Joseph arrived late in the evening the day before the census.

With every step on the dusty stone road, it felt as if a bolt of lightning shot up Joseph's spine. The pad of his heel felt flat and raw as though it was no longer there, like he was walking on the bone itself. Streaks of sweat ran down his legs through a layer of dust and dried blood which stained his skin, the result of a shortcut through some thorny bushes. But he was a strong man, persistent, and with God, he was able to endure each step.

In Joseph's hand he firmly held the leather reins of their donkey's bridle. The donkey's swaying steps were steady and strong but so was the pain that ripped through Mary's body. The weight of the child within her pressed down, making it hard to breathe and hard to endure. She needed to stop and find a place to rest.

The town was teeming with people. The streets were crowded even though it was late. The people, the noises, even the smells were offensive, but their journey was almost complete. They just needed to find a place to stay.

Joseph pushed against the flow of the crowd like a fish swimming upstream, looking for a sign with the letters "I-N-N" inscribed on it. Finally, there it was, a place to stay. He walked up the steps leading to the entry of the inn, put his hands on the iron latch, and lifted it to release the lock from the door's frame.

He turned around. "I'll just be a moment, sweetheart," he said, entering the building. Mary was still mounted on the donkey, her eyes closed, wincing from the pain in her back. She used one hand to rub the pain and the other was on her stomach, lifted high enough to signal, *okay*.

As Joseph stepped inside, he noticed it was just as densely populated as the street. He made his way up to the welcome counter to check in and get a room. "I would like a room, please," he said to the innkeeper.

"No rooms available here. Check down the road," the innkeeper said crassly, not even looking at Joseph.

A feeling of defeat rolled over Joseph, but he couldn't stop here. They continued to walk, just a little further down the road, and found another inn.

"Sorry, out of rooms," that innkeeper told Joseph. And another even further down the road, "Nope. All full."

The further down the road they walked, the fewer people that were in the streets, but the answer was still the same at every place—no room. Finally, they came to the last inn at the far edge of town. A man had walked out of the door and past Joseph, his eyebrows were low in a scowl of frustration. This was not a good sign.

Joseph opened the door and dragged himself up to the counter. He noticed mats on the floor of the welcome room where people were lying. This, too, was not a good sign. His head was telling him there were no rooms but his heart still had faith.

Lord God, please make a way for us, he prayed.

Joseph dropped his hand on the flat wooden counter, his head hung low, and his voice came out weak and tired, "Please, my wife is pregnant and we need a place to stay."

The innkeeper looked at Joseph with sympathy and said, "I am sorry, friend, but we have no rooms either. Everyone is here for *The Count*."

Joseph held back tears and said, "Please, there are no rooms left in all of Bethlehem, we'll take anything. We have been traveling for days and now I can't have my pregnant wife sleeping on the street."

The innkeeper received a glance of empathy from a woman, undoubtedly his wife, watching the interaction from across the room. With great compassion, the innkeeper placed his hand on Joseph's shoulder and said, "I know it's not much, but we had a helper sleep out in our stable and he said it was a great place to sleep. You are welcome to stay there. It's dry, there's fresh hay, and it's away from the street."

Relieved, Joseph raised his head and said, "That would be just fine, thank you." It was a thank you to both the innkeeper and God for an answered prayer.

Joseph turned around and walked out the door to tell Mary they had a place to stay. He saw she had dismounted from their donkey. She was facing away, her back to the inn, and hunched over. One hand was on the donkey's side to support her from falling over, and the other was holding her stomach. Joseph ran to her side.

"Mary, is everything alright?" he asked, his exhausted voice now filled with concern.

Mary was wincing in pain. "IT'S HAPPENING!"

LUKE 2:6-7

"6 While they were there, the time came for the baby to be born, 7 and she gave birth to her firstborn, a son. She wrapped him in cloths and placed him in a manger, because there was no guest room available for them."

DECEMBER 23
Jesus is Coming

Gabriel had been watching from Heaven. The three noblemen were on their way to Bethlehem, the young shepherd boy was excited and ready to travel down the mountain to celebrate and he helped Elias and Miriam fix their inn so there would be a place for Jesus to be born. He had followed God's commands perfectly and yet the outcome was not a celebration fit for a king, but rather for a lowly servant. So much time was spent preparing for this moment, ensuring there would be a safe and beautiful place for Joseph and Mary to stay. And yet the inn was full.

Gabriel turned his head sharply upward, his wings tensed with the possibility of disappointment and failure. He had always completed his tasks for God, but this time, so much was at stake. *Did I do something wrong?* he thought to himself. *The King of kings deserves more than a stable surrounded by animals, more than a bed of straw!*

"I know your heart, My faithful messenger," God said. **"But this has been the plan all along."**

Gabriel lowered his head to continue watching Mary and Joseph through the Eye. "The stable, my Lord? Shouldn't there be a palace made of gold and a feast to celebrate Jesus? All of Bethlehem, all of the WORLD should make room for Him."

God's voice was patient and filled with wisdom, **"I want Jesus to be born in the humblest of places then rise to glory as King to lead all those here in Heaven and on Earth. Jesus is a man just like them, and they too shall humble themselves before Me to enter My kingdom. Now go, welcome My Son to Earth, and sing songs of praise."**

A surge of joy overflowed through Gabriel from inside him. The Holy Spirit had entered into him and he immediately

understood the real task he was given—to listen to God, do as He asks, and spread the Good News. God would take care of the rest. He leapt from Heaven into the Eye, streaked across the sky like a comet into Bethlehem, and time stood still above the stable.

The light from within his spirit emanated around him, growing brighter and brighter. This was a new light, brighter than he had ever shown before. Gabriel was the star!

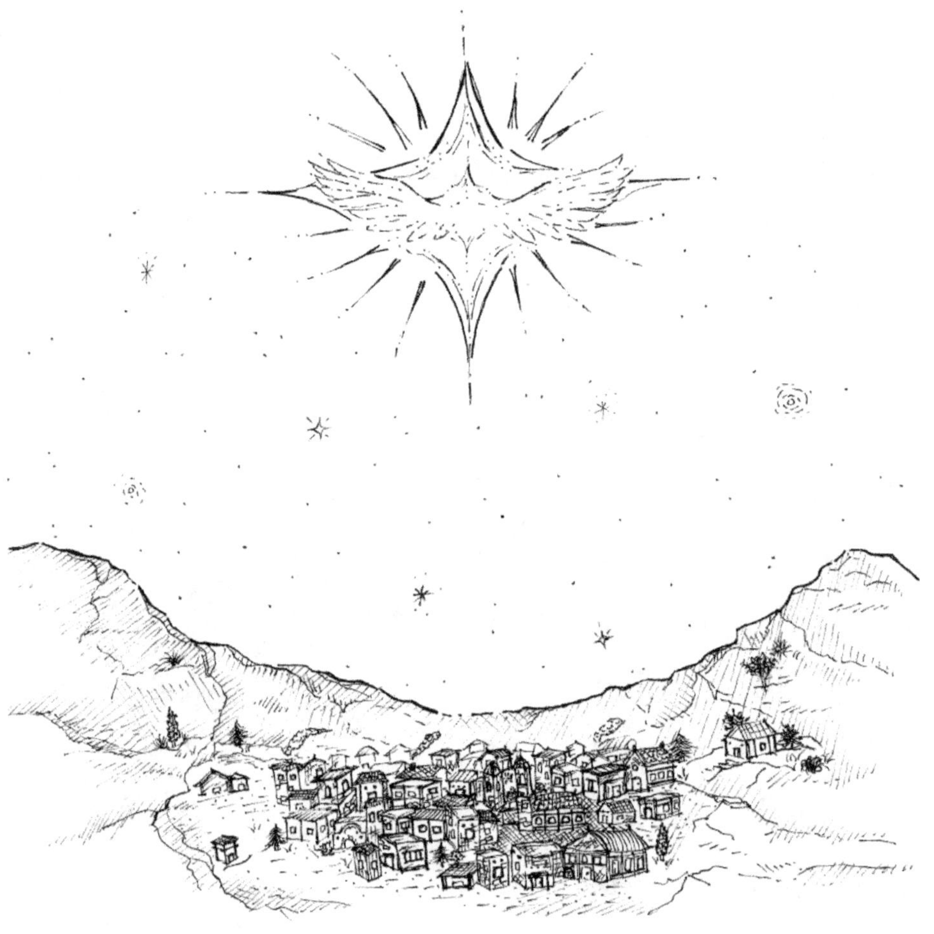

The same magnificent star he had shone to the noblemen in the desert a few nights before. Swirling light of bright shades of white and deep radiant purples and blues lit the way like a beacon to Jesus in the dark night sky.

The noblemen were miles away but they could see the light from Gabriel clearly. They were leaving King Herod's palace and traveling to Bethlehem to see Jesus.

From above, Gabriel began to sing. It started as a single voice, clear and strong:

O come, all ye faithful,
Joyful and triumphant!
O come ye, O come ye to Bethlehem;
Come and behold him
Born the King of Angels.

Then, all of Heaven answered:

O come, let us adore Him,
O come, let us adore Him,
O come, let us adore Him,
Christ the Lord!

Countless angels appeared, bursting across the sky like fireworks from Heaven, their wings slicing through the night in brilliant waves. They joined Gabriel's song, their voices blending into a magnificent, holy choir echoing across the hills.

Joshua, the young shepherd boy, heard the heavenly voices and saw the light from Gabriel pierce through his window. "It's time!" he exclaimed, stumbling to his feet. He ran out the door, grabbing his staff and a young lamb. The sky was dancing with light as he came to the edge of the mountain and shouted:

"Jesus is coming!"

LUKE 2:13-14

"[13] Suddenly a great company of the heavenly host appeared with the angel, praising God and saying, [14] 'Glory to God in the highest heaven, and on earth peace to those on whom his favor rests.'"

DECEMBER 24
A Holy Birth

Elias, the innkeeper, followed Joseph out from the welcome room to the front porch of the inn. The stables were down a dark path, so the innkeeper wanted to usher them safely and make sure they would be comfortable. The night was black, it was hard to see; only a few dim lanterns and the twinkling stars above lit the way. Joseph ran into the dark where his wife was waiting. Something was wrong.

Out of the darkness, he heard Joseph yell in a panic. "My wife is having the baby!"

Elias turned to his wife and said with urgency, "Miriam, grab towels and water and come down to the stables." He quickly ran out to help Joseph and led them to the stable.

Joseph wrapped his arms around Mary's waist and she around his neck. Every ounce of strength was poured into making sure she didn't fall as they walked down the dark path. One step at a time, they followed Elias. For the last week, the couple had walked a hundred miles. These last few steps were the hardest. The pain in Mary's stomach was great and intensified with every passing moment.

Elias opened the door to the stable and, as promised, clean hay carpeted the ground. Most of the stalls and pens were occupied by the animals brought in by the guests: large animals like oxen and donkeys, smaller ones like sheep and goats, and even smaller yet, chickens were all kept in the stable. In the back corner, a large stall still sat vacant; it was clean and private.

The innkeeper lit lanterns mounted on the walls and wooden posts. Then he collected as much of the hay as he could, as fast as he could, and made a makeshift bed for Mary. Joseph gently laid Mary down. He looked into her eyes, and said, "I love you."

Running into the stable with a pail of clean water and towels in hand, Miriam found the three. She looked around and saw something was missing. "We need a place for the baby to lie after he is born— we need a crib!" she told Elias. Elias grabbed a feeding trough, stuffed it with hay, and brought it back. "That's perfect!" she said as he sat it under the open window. "Okay, I will  take it from here," she said to the men, "go wait outside."

Joseph stood up, clinging to Mary's last touch, and said, "God is with you, and I will be right by the door." He backed up out of the stall and watched Mary lay there, wincing in pain.

Elias walked up to Joseph, grabbed his shoulder, and turned his body in the direction of the door, but his head still turned toward his wife. Finally, Elias was able to usher Joseph out of the stable and shut the door. The two men waited helplessly. They could hear Miriam giving Mary instructions to push, and Mary responded with a forceful grunt. Worried for his wife and newborn baby, Joseph began to pace back-and-forth in front of the stable.

Elias realized Joseph was anxious, so he tried to distract him with conversation. "So, what is the child's name?"

Joseph's fist was pressed to his lips, his gaze was straight out in front of him. "Uh… J-Jesus," he told the innkeeper with a gentle but swift voice.

"What a strong name, just like his father," he replied.

"You have no idea," Joseph responded quickly, moving his knuckle from the grip of his teeth.

Then the innkeeper felt a tug at his heart to start praying. He lifted his hands to Heaven and said, "Father God, You are the greatest Father and an example to us all. Please give this man the courage and wisdom to take care of Jesus as You care for us. Amen."

Joseph immediately stopped pacing. A sense of peace washed over him, filling his heart with solace.

In that moment, a bright light shined down like a spotlight from Heaven right over the stable and an angelic choir began to sing praises to God and the newborn King.

"Do you hear that?" the innkeeper asked.

"I certainly do," Joseph replied with his head tilted back and his eyes wide, taking in the glorious sight and sound of Heaven before him.

Not only was the night air filled with the sound of a heavenly choir, but the beautiful cry of a baby boy.

Joseph and Elias rushed into the stables where Mary had just given birth. She was lying there, right where he had left her. But now, wrapped in strips of cloth, nestled in her arms; Jesus! Joseph was awestruck and silent by the presence of this holy miracle. A light for generations to follow.

A short time later, three men dressed in nice clothes entered the stable. Joseph quickly jumped to his feet, and Elias followed. Their hearts pounded with a primal instinct to protect their families. "Who are you?" Joseph demanded, his voice no longer weary but firm and ready to defend.

"We are Balthazar, Melchior, and I am Caspar from the East," Caspar said calmly. "We have come to honor the baby King. We were visited by an angel and he told us to follow that star, which led us here to you."

Joseph simply responded with a name, "Gabriel?".

The name of the traveler from the desert, the name of the repairman that helped fix the inn, and of course, the name of the angel who visited both Mary and Joseph. Strangers until now, they had all been brought together by God's hand through Gabriel. A quiet hush rippled through the stable, everyone was stunned with awe.

Finally, Balthazar broke the silence. "It seems," he said with an affirming smile, "we are exactly where we're meant to be."

Joseph looked at Mary then back at the three men. "Please, come in and join us," he said.

Mary smiled as she gazed upon her baby peacefully sleeping in her arms. Carefully, she handed Him to Joseph who laid Him gently in the makeshift crib beneath the window for their visitors to see.

The three men approached the baby one at a time, each holding something in their hands. Caspar was the first to kneel at the manger, "What is His name?" he asked, staring at the perfect baby boy.

"He is our Immanuel, Jesus!" Mary responded, unable to contain her smile.

Caspar continued, filled with gratitude and joy, "I present to You, Lord Jesus, myrrh. For You are our Savior from sin." He set down a beautifully etched clay jar and reverently bowed his head. After a moment, he lifted himself off the ground and made room for the others.

Balthazar walked up next and also knelt, "Lord Jesus, I bring you, frankincense. For You are God the Son." He laid down an intricately carved wooden box next to the jar then stood back.

Finally, Melchior approached carrying a small chest, also wooden but inlaid with gold and turquoise. His eyes filled with tears. "Lord Jesus, please forgive me," he said as both knees hit the ground. His eyes hung low with shame, pulling his forehead to the hay. "I have only been concerned with my wealth and my knowledge; I am a man of this world. I want to give You that which controls me, and I wish to be freed of my sins. You are Lord God, Savior, and King. Please accept my gift." He lifted his head off the ground and set the box next to the other gifts. He opened the lid—gold!

Mary and Joseph were overwhelmed with emotion. They felt so honored to have the three noblemen and the innkeepers there to celebrate their baby, Jesus. But then another approached, a young boy holding a lamb.

"Excuse me," the boy said shyly, "I have also come to worship this baby, our Messiah, and wanted to bring you this lamb as a gift. He is a Shepherd of man and we will all be His sheep. Praise be to God!" He set the young lamb down on the hay covered floor and smiled.

Mary's motherly instincts kicked in, and she went over to the young boy and gave him a long heartfelt embrace. "Thank you. You are so sweet," she said, kissing the top of his head. Then she turned and knelt beside Jesus who was still lying in the manger. She picked Him up and cradled Him in her arms and softly said, "We will forever celebrate Your name on this day.

HAPPY BIRTHDAY, JESUS!"

ISAIAH 42:1

"Here is my servant, whom I uphold, my chosen one in whom I delight; I will put my Spirit on him, and he will bring justice to the nations."

DECEMBER 25
Jesus the Messiah

Jesus was born, the Heavens sang, and his tasks were complete. Gabriel sat on his favorite spot atop the highest mountain where the breeze blew softly and made the grass dance. The air was clean and the view of Earth was perfect. But Gabriel still had a question: *why*?

"Because I love them," God said. "My Son is with them, not in power, not in majesty, but in humility. Jesus will be an example of how to glorify Me:

He is born as one of them, among the poor and lowly, and He will grow in wisdom and truth.

He is compassionate and will feed thousands when there is no food.

He is kind and will restore sight to the blind.

He is caring and will heal the sick, injured, and lame.

He is strong and will control storms and water in ways people have never seen.

He is loving and will raise people from the dead.

He is forgiving; He will die at the hands of the sinful, then rise from the grave to live and rule in Heaven forever. Anyone who believes this and is sorry for their sinful ways will also be welcome here forever.

He is the ultimate sacrifice, and it will pain Me to see Him suffer. But after it is finished, I will do anything for those who believe in Him.

For now, let's just enjoy this moment."

MERRY CHRISTMAS

ROMANS 10:9

"If you declare with your mouth, "Jesus is Lord," and believe in your heart that God raised him from the dead, you will be saved."

UNWRAPPED

This book was really fun to write and I hope it brought you just as much joy to read it. I also hope you enjoyed it enough to make reading it a tradition every year. As you read through the story, there are a few hidden "presents" I left for you—did you find them? If you didn't, that's fine, but I want to unwrap them for you here.

CHAPTER 1

- I start off describing Heaven, but did you notice something special about the first paragraph? Every fruit of the spirit is listed there. Galatians 5:22-23 says: "22 But the fruit of the Spirit is love, joy, peace, [patience], kindness, goodness, faithfulness, 23 gentleness and self-control. Against such things there is no law."

- I also describe the city as having golden streets just like it says in Revelation 21:21.

- Mathew 6:10 is the verse where Jesus describes the best way to pray—it's the Lord's Prayer. One of the lines in this prayer is also present in the story, "His will be done on Earth as it is in Heaven."

- There are many instances in the Bible that reference Jesus as being "the seed". I invite you to look up all the different uses. Genesis 3:15 is the very first prophecy about Jesus: "And I will put enmity between you and the woman, and between your seed and her seed; He shall bruise your head, and you shall bruise His heel." Here, the "seed of the woman" is understood to be Jesus, who would defeat Satan.

- God never forces his will on Mary, but rather He says, "If she is willing." This is very important to show God gives all of us freewill.

CHAPTER 2

- We don't know for sure where Mary was when Gabriel appeared to her. Some traditional theories say she was at home. Here I placed her praying in a garden. This plays into Jesus being a seed and God being a gardener concept.

- The garden is also a "slice of Heaven" for Mary. You can see that there are some similarities in how I described them. Also, I reference "felt like home" to satisfy the previous point.

- Little known fact, not only was Joseph from the lineage of King David, Mary was too. This is why I say, "the Messiah that was promised to you and your family".

- Again, God does not force His will on us, and Mary says "Let His will be done!" In that moment is when the Holy Spirit came upon her.

CHAPTER 3

- This is the first time we hear Mary's prayer. There are many little prayers in the story to help show how simple it is to pray and put God first in every situation. Mary says, "I don't want to hurt him, but this is Your will." She is putting God first above her own desires.

- We know Joseph was a carpenter because of Matthew 13:55, Jesus also practiced the same trade as illustrated in Mark 6:3. It is a humble, hard-working trade that prepared Jesus for a life of service.

CHAPTER 4

- I take you back in time to when David was but a shepherd boy. This illustrates God's ability to move beyond the construct of time. This is how we know we are victorious over Satan; He can see the end.
- David tossing stones is a nod to the David and Goliath story (1 Samuel 17).
- Did you catch when David said, "You scared me" and Gabriel responded, "I've gotten that a lot lately"? This is Gabriel thinking about his approach to Mary—BEHOLD!
- "It's hard work being a shepherd." Will come up again in chapter 18 and 19.
- David is said to be the author of the Psalms. This is the reference to poetry and music.
- David is also telling Gabriel stories about killing beasts to save his beloved sheep. This is also in the Bible; 1 Samuel 17:34-37.

- I used Gabriel's angelic brilliance as a way to communicate to the prophet Samuel. Only he could see this and made for an easy message—just put David in the spotlight.

CHAPTER 5

- We move ahead 30 years when David is now King. David really wants to build the temple for God. Although David repented, he was pretty sinful. So, God didn't want him to build the temple. His son Solomon would do this when he became king.
- This is the whole premise of the story—God's promise to David called, the "Davidic covenant". God promises David his dynasty will last forever, one of his descendants will always be on the throne, and ultimately, points forward to the coming of the Messiah (Jesus), who is called the "Son of David" in the New Testament.
- Gabriel isn't necessarily the angel who delivered this message to Nathan, but it fit the story really nicely.

CHAPTER 6

- I have shifted the timeline a bit here, obviously we are back at "current day" for Joseph. But even more so, Joseph didn't think about divorcing from Mary until after her visit with Elizabeth when he notices Mary is pregnant, "She was *found* to be pregnant by the Holy Spirit." (Matthew 1:18)
- Joseph is visited by an angel. In the Bible it does not specifically say it was Gabriel, but here I have placed Gabriel to tie the story together.
- Furthermore, Joseph is visited by an angel in a dream. The beginning of the chapter is supposed to show Joseph working himself to exhaustion and falls asleep without our knowing. At the end of the chapter is when it reveals he slept through the night.

CHAPTER 7

- Elizabeth is six months pregnant at this point in the story (and in the Bible, Luke 1:26) this is key for chapter 9.

- When Mary enters Elizabeth and Zechariah's home, Elizabeth says, "even my little one in my belly is jumping for joy…" this is derived from Luke 1:41.

CHAPTER 8

- You may have already questioned this; Why did I use Zechariah? Your Bible may say "Zacharias". Older translations of the Bible use Zacharias, while modern Bibles (I am using the NIV) have Zechariah. Same person though.
- I loved the idea of telling Mary about Elizabeth's pregnancy through the writing of Zechariah. It made for dynamic storytelling, and I even put in a little humor.
- What does it mean when we say John "prepared the way for Jesus"? In Isaiah 40:3 it says, "A voice of one calling: 'In the wilderness prepare the way for the Lord; make straight in the desert a highway for our God.'" Then Gabriel tells Zechariah that his son John will "make ready a people prepared for the Lord." (Luke 1:16-17) John was a man of the wilderness wearing camel's hair and a leather belt around his

waist, who ate only locusts and wild honey. He himself says, "I am the voice of one calling in the wilderness, 'Make straight the way for the Lord.'" in John 1:23. I believe the preparation was for Jesus to be baptized in the desert with water as an example of what we need to do.

CHAPTER 9

- This may be controversial, but I believe Mary was still staying with Elizabeth and Zechariah when John was born. The Bible never says when Mary left, in fact Luke 1:58 says, "[Elizabeth's] neighbors and *relatives* heard that the Lord had shown her great mercy, and they shared her joy." Just two verses before that (56) it says, "Mary stayed with Elizabeth for about three months and then returned home. Are you telling me she stayed with her favorite cousin until she was about to give birth, then leave just before? That would be so surprising. So, was she there or, was she not? We do not know for certain, but it is fun to think she was and she saw the miracle that was John being born.

- Mary is singing psalms to Elizabeth of which were written by King David, the same King David from chapters 4 and 5.

- In this time, it was customary for men to not be in the room during the birth of a child.

- Couple of things with Zechariah getting his voice back: 1 It did not happen on the day John was born and 2 He wrote John's name first, then he was able to talk. His first words were in praise of God.

CHAPTER 10

- Here I am depicting Caesar Augustus as mean and power hungry. He was definitely a powerful ruler and cared about expanding his empire, but he was also very concerned about stabilizing the empire. As long as the people, Jew or otherwise, paid taxes and didn't cause rebellion, he tolerated their local traditions.

- Without Caesar's drive to want to expand and collect taxes, the census would have never happened. The Messiah had to be born in Bethlehem (Micah 5:2). Everything is good with God's timing!

- The coin illustration is from that of a Julius Caesar coin. Notice it says, "Caesar"? The actual coin says "CAESAR DICT PERPETVO" ("Caesar, dictator for life")

- The family lineage for Augustus is a bit strange. Augustus was the grand-nephew of Julius Caesar — his mother was Julius Caesar's niece. Julius Caesar didn't have any children, so in his will, he adopted Augustus as his son and heir. That made Augustus Julius Caesar's son by Roman law, even though by blood he was Caesar's great-nephew.

CHAPTER 11

- Again, Mary was gone for three months, likely showing at this point. Canonically in the Bible, this is when Joseph would see Mary and realize she was pregnant (Matthew 1:18), leading to him wanting to divorce her, but then Gabriel comes to him in the dream, where he ultimately accepts Jesus as his son.

- This chapter gave me a chance to bring in the words of Jesus. There are many things we pick up from our parents, either intentionally or involuntary. I liked the idea that Jesus may have heard Mary say, "I would forgive you seventy times seven times." And it stuck with Him, telling his disciples later in his ministry.

CHAPTER 12

- We shift forward in time and Mary is now more than eight months pregnant—a critical time in a pregnancy. It is the night before leaving on their journey. It would take about seven days to walk to Bethlehem from Nazareth. This is why Joseph gets worried. He wants to provide for Mary and Jesus, but he is not in control. She will most likely give birth while they are away. Mary is a great wife and helper and shows Joseph not to be worried. Yes, it may be hard, yes, it may be uncomfortable. But God is with us, so why worry?

CHAPTER 13

- Whenever my wife and I go on vacation, it is a running joke that I forget something, but my wife is always there to help me remember. Having fun in a marriage is important, laugh at yourself, but always have God first.

- Gabriel has been out of the story for a few chapters now. I believe we have angels around us or watching us all the time, but they do not necessarily intervene at every step.

- Now we transition to the second half of the story– the other side. God now tells Gabriel to setup a spectacular celebration and I introduce three more tasks for him; the wise men (noble men), Innkeeper, and the shepherd. I loved writing from these different perspectives and I hope you enjoyed reading how the nativity story might have developed in real life.

CHAPTER 14

- Up to this point, Gabriel has really stuck to his angel abilities. I wanted to show that angels may approach you in different ways: supernaturally like through dreams or visions, but also physically.

- The three noble men are a reflection of us. We are generally focused on wealth here on Earth and trying to be head-smart, rather than building our wealth in Heaven from the fruits of our actions, and being smart in the ways of God and Jesus.

- Traditionally we refer to the three traveling men in the desert as the *"three wise men"*. In this book, I only refer to them as the "Noblemen", with the exception of Melchior and King Herod (as you will see later). They are the only two characters that use the term, "Wise Men". Melchior is a proud, worldly man and thinks highly of himself, this will be broken down a bit later in the story. And King Herod uses it as a way to mock them.

CHAPTER 15

- Remember kids, even royalty have a bedtime routine.
- The inscription on the side of the manger (INRI) was to be a foreshadow to Jesus's crucifixion. It is the Latin abbreviation for the charge written above Jesus on the cross. It stands for:
    o I → Iesus = Jesus
    o N → Nazarenus = of Nazareth

      o R → Rex = King

      o I → Iudaeorum = of the Jews

So together:

"Iesus Nazarenus Rex Iudaeorum" = "Jesus of Nazareth, King of the Jews."

CHAPTER 16

- After the three noblemen shared the same dream Melchior starts to question his faith. While the other two seem to be more open to the idea of God and the supernatural, he is more stubborn.

- Originally, I included a lot of geographically accurate information in the story but it became distracting, so, I will expand on it here. Bethlehem was about 6 miles south of Jerusalem and Nazareth was about 65 miles north of Jerusalem. Think about all the travel these people did between these three places. How long does it take you to walk a mile?

- The quote from Isiaha is so powerful because it is a prophecy written in the 8th century before Jesus was born. "The virgin will conceive and give birth to a son, and will call him Immanuel."

CHAPTER 17

- King Herod ruled over five main territories; Judea (with Jerusalem, Bethlehem, Jericho, etc.), Samaria, Galilee (which included Nazareth), Perea, and Idumea. Jerusalem was Herod's capital.

- His official title given to him by the Romans was "King of the Jews". You will see many historians refer to him as "Herod the Great" because of his power, accomplishments, and wide rule over multiple territories.

- Again, this is the only other place in the story where the term "Wise Men" is used and it is used as a way to mock the three noblemen. It is part of the transition for Melchior especially. His own words are used against him to belittle him, until he humbles himself before Christ, which he will, later in the story.

- To seek the truth is to seek Jesus.

- Notice when they leave Jerusalem, the sky is dancing. The story suggests, Jesus was just born and the angels were singing at this point. But in the Bible, it never specifies when the wisemen come to present gifts to Jesus. Some say as early as a few days after Jesus's birth and others say up to two years because of Matthew 2:16, "...[Herod] gave orders to kill all the boys in Bethlehem and its vicinity who were *two years old* and under, in accordance with the time he had learned from the Magi."

- The quote used to complete the chapter perfectly illustrates what was happening in that moment for the noblemen, however verse two was struck from this book due to its graphic nature.

CHAPTER 18

- Joshua laying on the ground using a rock as a pillow is a reference to Jacob dreaming about a stairway to Heaven in Genesus 28:11.
- In the Biblical timeline, "an angel of the Lord" (not specifically Gabriel) appears to more than one shepherd in the fields bringing the good news of Jesus's birth. Not just Gabriel and one young shepherd boy as it is in this story.

- The young shepherd boy's name I chose was Joshua which means, "The Lord is salvation". Jesus and Joshua are the same name. In Hebrew it is pronounced, Yeshua.

- I tried to expand on the story of the lost sheep here found in Matthew 18:12. Jesus is missing from Joshua's life.

CHAPTER 19

- "It's hard work being a shepherd" is a phrase Gabriel heard from David in chapter 4. Gabriel remembers this and uses it as a way to show his angelic power.

- Originally, (in the story) Gabriel was going to ask Joshua to bring his drum when he heard the choir of angels. But this seemed too cheesy, even for me... and I like cheese!

CHAPTER 20

- Everything in this chapter is made up, we know nothing about the innkeeper so this gave me the freedom to really think about what was happening from the innkeeper's perspective.

- The name Elias means, "The Lord is my God."

- The name Miriam is the original Hebrew form of Mary.

- Elias has a similar mannerism to Joseph in that he wants to provide and be the best man for his wife, but he does so with anxiety and worry. This is why we need our beautiful wives to help balance us out. They are strong emotionally and can calm us down just as Miriam does for Elias and Mary for Joseph.

- It was important for me to show the innkeeper's struggle and give a reason for Gabriel to come and prepare a room for Mary and Joseph.

- God loves to create, make things beautiful, and see things through to completion. This gives Gabriel an opening to talk to Elias about helping him restore his inn. This is not just a rebuild of a building but also a rebuild of Elias's faith in God.

- We all have our gifts to share. No matter how small you may think they are, your gift is big in the eyes of God; use them for His Kingdom!

- Gabriel sleeping in the stable and saying that he "sleeps like a baby" is totally intentional. Although Gabriel may not know it yet.

- All the praise of good works should always go to God-
including this very book. I feel so honored to have
written it.

CHAPTER 21

- This was a fun chapter to write! It really highlights
the faith Miriam has in God. She had one coin that
was worth but a slice of bread and she set off to use
that last coin. She expected to go to the market and
return with a roast but instead, God placed that
little boy there for her to help, and she returned
with a whole group of people to stay at their inn.
- The name Tobias was intentionally selected because
it means, "God is good."
- The baker tore a piece of bread which should bring
thoughts of Jesus at the last supper.
- Any success we may have, the answer of 'Who?'
should always be God!
- "With God, all things are possible" is directly pulled
from scripture in two places; Matthew 19:26 and
Mark 10:27. Both referencing Jesus talking about the
wealthy entering Heaven. "It is easier for a camel to

go through the eye of a needle than for someone who is rich to enter the kingdom of God." Mark 10:25.

- The last few paragraphs of the chapter end with who we know is Joseph and Mary.

CHAPTER 22

- Joseph and Mary traveled more than 70 miles from Nazareth to Bethlehem. Imagine walking 5 hours for 7 days straight across difficult terrain and being pregnant. That would make me tired and want to rest my feet anywhere I could.

- In many circles, it is believed Mary and Joseph were poor. I don't think they were well off or rich by any means but I believe they had enough money to pay for a room, there was just no rooms available for them.

- At the end we see the timeline of the previous chapter line up. In this chapter we as the readers assume the innkeepers are Elias and Miriam.

- If you compare the dialog between chapter 21 and 22, you will notice they are not perfectly aligned. This was intentional! I wanted to highlight the fact that the meaning of the story is still relevant even though the words may not be exact. We see this in the Gospels. As a previously mentioned example, in Mark 10:27 the verse reads, "Jesus looked at them and said, 'With man this is impossible, but not with God; all things are possible with God.'" But in Luke 18:27 it reads a little different, "Jesus replied, 'What is impossible with man is possible with God.'". Both are from the same context and mean the same thing.

CHAPTER 23

- God is the all-powerful living God that knows all things and outcomes. He uses angels and people to accomplish His will. But there is no one, other than God Himself, that knows what will happen and how. Angels do have a leg up but even they may not know every detail.

- I love that God came down from Heaven and was born in the lowest-of-lows, out with the animals, and in the end, he rose from the dead to be in Glory as the King of all things.

- We can learn from Gabriel's lesson, our task from God is clear and simple; Listen to God, do as He asks, and spread the Good News of Jesus. In the end, Gabriel was the "star" that led everybody to Jesus (this is my interpretation).

- I hope I was able to spur a bit of praise and worship in your house singing, "Oh Come All Ye Faithful." At first it may seem awkward but every year you do it, the anticipation of that moment *will* bring joy to your family.

- As mentioned in chapter 18's unwrapped section, the Bible says that an angel appeared to a *group* of shepherds, then a "great company of heavenly hosts" began "Praising God." The angel and the heavenly host do not explicitly break out in song, but because they "Praised God", we assume this was a song. They say, "Glory to God in the highest heaven, and on earth peace to those on whom his favor rests." (Luke 2:8–14)

CHAPTER 24

- The moment we have all been waiting for, the buildup of the entire story—Jesus's birth! This chapter was intentionally longer than most of the others so you can spend time with one another on the highly anticipated night before Christmas.

- Joseph clearly loves Mary and I hope that was apparent throughout the story. His love and devotion to both Mary and God alike is a model in which the men of our current day household should pull from.

- As mentioned earlier, the men would not have been in the same room as Mary as she was giving birth, per the custom of the day.

- Anybody else think Jesus is a strong name (like His *Father's*)?

- I have heard the term "biblical triangulation" before and thought I would bring in an instance of showing how that is practically done here. If you take three or more disparate sources and they are all saying the same thing, this is a good indication of truth.

- Immanuel is a Hebrew name that means: "God with us." It appears in the Bible as a prophecy about the coming Messiah from Isaiah 7:14: "Therefore the Lord himself will give you a sign: The virgin will conceive and give birth to a son, and will call him Immanuel."

- It was powerful to write the moment the three wise men lay down their gifts. The symbolism of each of the gifts and the sub story of Melchior putting down the thing he idolized most, his gold. Just a recap of the symbolism:
  - Gold represents royalty, a gift for a king.
  - Frankincense represents divinity and Jesus's priestly role.
  - Myrrh was used for burial and embalming, foreshadowing Jesus's suffering and death for us.
- The shepherd boy bringing a lamb is a symbol of Jesus being the Lamb of God and being the sacrifice for us all.

CHAPTER 25

- This is also a nod to how angels do what they are asked, and may not know the plan in its entirety, but God will reveal His plan in *His* time.

- In John 19:30 Jesus is hanging on the cross and says, "It is **finished**", then He gives up His Spirit. God knows the beginning and the end. This is why we, as Christians, are confident/have faith of the victory against evil.

- This is the grand finale with beautiful illustrations from Ariana Madison. Though short, it is rich in Bible verses, which I highly encourage you to read. Most of this chapter was already discussed throughout the story but with some finer detail. Matthew 11:4-5 "Go back and report to John what you hear and see: The blind receive sight, the lame walk, those who have leprosy are cleansed, the deaf hear, the dead are raised, and the good news is proclaimed to the poor."
    - o Feeding thousands
        - Matthew 14:13-21
        - Mark 6:30-44

- Luke 9:10-17
- John 6:1-14
- Restoring sight
    - Luke 18:35-43
    - Matthew 9:27-31
    - Mark 8:22-26
    - John 9:1-12
- Healing the sick
    - Matthew 4:23-24
    - Luke 4:40
- Healing the paralyzed
    - Matthew 9:1-8
    - John 5:1-15
    - Luke 5:17-26
- Controlling storms
    - Matthew 8:23-27
    - Mark 4:35-41
    - Luke 8:22-25
- Jesus's first miracle turning water into wine
    - John 2:1-11
- Jesus raising people from the dead
    - Mark 5:21-24, 35-43
    - Luke 7:11-17

- - John 11:1-44
  - o Jesus dying on the cross for us
    - - Matthew 28:1-10
    - - Mark 16:1-8
    - - Luke 24:1-12
    - - John 20:1-18

There is so much more to learn about and read about our amazing Lord and Savior, Jesus Christ in the Bible. He is the reason we celebrate Christmas. It was such an honor to write this story and thank you for reading it. I pray you are blessed by this and you seek more of Him in everything you do

IF YOU ENJOYED THE SOTRY...

... I would love your help getting copies into the hands of as many families as possible. My goal is to help spur early reading, relationship building, family time, and above all, a desire to learn more about our Lord and Savior, Jesus Christ. I feel this book could be a catalyst for that. If you could find it in your heart, please:

- **Write a review** on the platform you purchased this book this from.

- **Upvote other reviews.** This helps feature reviews that best describe your experience and will hopefully help others decide to buy it too.

- **Purchase a copy** for a friend or relative. They would make great party favors for your *Thanksgiving* guests.

- **Purchase in Bulk or Wholesale.** Please go to the Website and connect with the publisher to get a discounted offer.

- **Post on social media** and be sure to tag the book's page.
  - o **Facebook** - @ThePromiseOfBethlehem
  - o **X** - @PromiseOfBethlm
  - o **Instagram** - @ThePromiseOfBethlehem

- **Send an email.** I would love to hear your comments
  - o contact@thepromiseofbethlehem.com

- **Let your church know.** Tell a pastor what this book meant to you and your testimony.

- **Write a letter.** I would love to receive a letter or see any colored in copies of the illustrations. I will even post some on the website.

SchockWave Publishing Co, LLC.
975 E Riggs Rd
Ste 12-308
Chandler, AZ 85249 USA

- **Visit the website to learn more about our mission.** Continue to check back at the website. I will be adding more content as the book grows. There is a page dedicated to each member of the family. It is also another easy place to reach out to me. With the "contact us" page, you can tell me what you thought of the book or how it has helped you get closer to Jesus. And lastly, if you need prayer, we would love to do that for you as well.

https://thepromiseofbethlehem.com/